S0-BBR-671

A Wonderful Story
(with a super-happy ending!)

"It's deep deep, tender, moving, and full of wonderful zappy wit...above all it spoke to me—about loving, a special kind of loving for women. I don't usually like happy endings, but this one is great...perfect. Her best book."
SUE KAUFMAN

A Lovely Story
(about a woman and the man she loves!)

"This is the first truly funny book about neurotic women trying to find love in their lives and meaning in their work...Brilliant and poignant." *PLAYBOY*

A Lovely Story
(about a man and the woman he loves!)

"When it's not laugh-out-loud funny, it's deeply touching—a very nice job indeed." IRA LEVIN

Final Analysis

Lois Gould

 AVON
PUBLISHERS OF BARD, CAMELOT, DISCUS, EQUINOX AND FLARE BOOKS

AVON BOOKS
A division of
The Hearst Corporation
959 Eighth Avenue
New York, New York 10019

Copyright © 1974 by Lois Gould.
Published by arrangement with Random House, Inc.
Library of Congress Catalog Card Number: 73-18304.

ISBN 0-380-00234-5

First Avon Printing, February, 1975.

AVON TRADEMARK REG. U.S. PAT. OFF. AND
FOREIGN COUNTRIES, REGISTERED TRADEMARK—
MARCA REGISTRADA, HECHO EN CHICAGO, U.S.A.

Printed in the U.S.A.

FOR ROBERT
AND THE MEMORY OF
ILONA FOLDES, WHO LOVED HIM

The lover in these poems
is me;
the doctor,
Love.
He appears
as husband, lover
analyst & muse,
as father, son
& maybe even God
& surely death.

All this is true.

The man you turn to
in the dark
is many men.

This is an open secret
women share
& yet agree to hide
as if
they might then
hide it from themselves.

I will not hide.

I write in the nude.
I name names.
I am I.
The doctor's name is Love.

> "Autobiographical"
> by Erica Jong

Chapter

ONE

HE PRONOUNCED HER crazy inside of nine minutes. Actually, he didn't pronounce it so much as yell it at her. "Crazy!" She should never have told him how she happened to call him for the appointment.

"Well." She tried a defensive shrug. "What do you expect from a crazy person who needs a crazy doctor?" She smiled hard, to make up for everything.

There was still a chance he would find her irresistibly witty and unconventional. Gay madcap comedy starring a young Katharine Hepburn at the peak of her form. Maybe he was already smitten by the excellent posture. She carried herself like an extravagant birthday present. Strange men would never suspect that inside was this incredible snapping brain. But could she fool a psychiatrist? A *trained* psychiatrist? She pictured a bearded Viennese flea in spangled tights, precariously balanced.

Dr. Foxx studied her briefly before smiling back. A careful smile, his. Moderately reassuring yet firmly detached. A smile like an analytic hour.

"Bites nails below quick," he jotted in his clean spiral note pad.

As a matter of fact, she failed to see what was so crazy about how she picked him. She had made an exhaustive New York psychiatrist list with the help of an off-duty Crisis Intervention Center aide she happened to meet last Saturday in an out-of-order phone booth on East 57th Street. Lists were a hobby of his too. He already had maybe two hundred psychiatrists listed according to East and West Side; Jewish and nonsectarian; over 40 and under; over 40 *dollars* and under; black, white and other; male, female and other; not to mention alphabetical order. It took her three days just to narrow the field down to East Side nonsectarian white males under 40 and under $40, with a special * notation indicating possible lower clinic rates for cases that were both needy and "interesting." The Crisis Intervention man had thought she would definitely qualify as "interesting" (single, female, articulate, attractive, $115-a-week magazine job, solid Midwest family that still sent a moist tomato-soup cake along with the worried monthly letter).

What finally cinched it for S. Conrad Foxx, M.D., was that she felt sorry for any boy whose S. had been worse than his Conrad. Maybe that was the crazy part. But she hadn't *told* him that part.

On the telephone Dr. Foxx had not asked what she thought her problem might be. Since that was kind of him, she volunteered that her age was twenty-eight, which was only a year and a half less than true. She also mentioned that twenty-eight seemed as good a point as any to hang up a person's shoes, or gun or skates or chips or towel, as the case might be. Permanently retiring your sweat-stained number rather than waiting for it to come up by itself. If you let it go at twenty-eight, someone might just—in lieu of flowers—play the single white baby spot across the otherwise darkened stage, following the playful ghost of your perfectly disciplined body's legendary fluid movements. And there'd be a standing ovation for all that you might have, if only . . .

Dr. Foxx's waiting room was a small box with three doors, permitting the landlord to call the apartment a three with gracious entry foyer. An old rotating fan whirred noisily in one corner, although it was January and freezing. She suddenly realized that he must keep it going not to stir the air, but to muffle any cry of anguish that might seep through the cracks in the soundproof door. Other doctors, she had heard, piped André Kostelanetz in through hidden stereo speakers, and a few had white-sound machines imitating the ocean. She liked the old fan; somehow it went better with the S. Conrad.

While waiting, she thoughtfully composed a detailed personal history for him, including dates of most recent vaccination and eye tests, hereditary allergies and recurring illogical fears. Most Dreaded Disease: puerperal fever. Most Feared Act of Violence: multiple stab wounds inflicted by undertipped United Parcel man. Miscellaneous Fears: loss of control over lower facial muscles; insanity leading to gross neglect of unsightly hairs; overflowing toilet in public ladies' room; fainting in better-dress department while wearing sweater with armhole stains marked not removable by dry cleaner.

At the last minute she crossed out the part about Lifelong Ambition: serious writer. First of all, he couldn't possibly help with that. A person who was twenty-eight (or even thirty) and had a decent job in her chosen field did not get to crab about "serious." Doctors only cared about "functioning in work." She sighed. Lifelong Ambition: functioning ...

When Dr. Foxx opened the door, she crumpled the unfinished list into her coat pocket, on the off chance that he might ask her to empty the contents of her purse on his desk. That was another fear to list under Miscellaneous.

She had resolved that during the first session she would tell him only the shameful secrets that would definitely qualify her as interesting rather than disgusting. The pain and bleeding during sexual intercourse might be okay, but not the kinky fantasies. Not that she had definite preferences among obscene telephone calls, and certainly not that in the second drawer, in the right sleeve of her red pajamas, she kept thirty-one post cards showing nuns raptly submitting to thirty-one sexual indignities with small men of Hispanic persuasion.

Obviously she would have to start with the high school memory book. Squarely in the eye she would let him have the fact that there had been no wrist corsages, not a one, and no letters whatsoever referring to anyone's darling. She would simply tell him that this book, which she could certainly bring in if he insisted, for any reason, contained a large collection of dirt samples scraped from the soles of her cousin Cynthia's boy friends' basketball shoes. Also an assortment of cigarette butts clearly identified with the name and physical description of every blind date who never called again. On the last page of this book—well, maybe she could tear that out—was a *Daily News* centerfold picture of Burton F. Bigelow, the young mass-rape-slayer, showing him smiling at the piano just prior to his execution. The caption read "Burton F. Bigelow practices Beethoven while waiting to be hanged."

After the first fifteen minutes, though, she noticed that Dr. Foxx had stopped jotting in his note pad. He seemed to be gazing intently out the window at a policeman ticketing cars with MD license plates. See, she thought. What happens when you pay thirty-five dollars an hour is that you're still boring.

Maybe if she told him about Norma. "This girl named Norma," she plunged in recklessly, "in camp—"

"Excuse me," said Dr. Foxx, flashing this beautiful, really *beautiful*, smile, and bolting so abruptly from his swivel chair that it was still shuddering slightly when he returned, flushed with triumph, a full four minutes later by her watch. If Dr. Foxx charges thirty-five dollars for a forty-five-minute hour, she was calculating, how much is four minutes . . .

Of course, he had undoubtedly rushed out to tell the policeman that the owner of license plate 4 MD 316, a shabby-looking VW bug, indicating sincerity, was parked there on an emergency basis while treating a suicidal pregnant blond teenaged underground movie starlet whose father happened to play squash with the Police Commissioner every Thursday.

"Norma?" he prompted, settling back into the chair. "In camp?"

"Norma?" she echoed icily. "Oh, that."

"Well?"

She considered not telling. Sullen, he would write. Uncooperative, uninteresting, inarticulate and not really attractive.

"Norma," she said, "was standing in the doorway watching me, that's all."

"How long was she watching you?"

"How should I know? All I remember is how all of a sudden she started shrieking at me. Norma had this triumphant piercing shriek, if you can picture it, *'Take your finger out of your—'* "

"Your . . . ?" He leaned forward.

"Nose, I think."

"But it could just as easily have been . . . ?"

"Oh, sure. Just as easily."

"And you still think about it?"

"Constantly," she said. "To this day whenever I put my finger in anything, I think of Norma."

Dr. Foxx sat back, sighing faintly, and sheathed

his ballpoint. "What made you decide to call me?" he demanded.

She burst at once into tears. S. Conrad *Ratt*, you mean, she raged silently. She should have known from the color of his waiting room. Brown that might as well be green, or vice versa. She should have guessed from the minute he opened the door, with his short socks inching down into his dusty shoes and the short sleeves on his summer shirt flapping out sharply from his nice tan arms like stubby permanent-press wings. So what if he had so much thick sandy hair that he would never be bald, and beautiful multicolored eyes? She would bet he couldn't touch her worst score on "Word Power" in the *New York Post* ("Find at least 57 five-letter words in IMBRI-CATED SNOUT BEETLE, a destructive insect. Answers tomorrow").

"Kleenex?" he said, nodding at the box that was thoughtfully provided near her right elbow. She wondered how much a psychiatrist could reasonably deduct a year for Kleenex. "What upset you just now?" he prodded gently, uncapping the ballpoint.

I . . . Despise . . . You. She wanted to fling it carelessly over her shoulder like a pastel scarf, just as she reached the door. "I don't know" was what she said, however. And went on sniffling into his deductible Kleenex.

"I see," he replied, jotting thoughtfully.

He sees, she thought wildly. This one-way mirror permits the professional observer to evaluate at first hand each child's pattern of destructive behavior, without, of course, the child's slightest inkling that there is an adult presence in the room.

There was absolutely no way to toss a wet tissue into his wastebasket from where she was sitting. If she tried, it would hit him in the knee, and God knew what he would write about her then. On the other hand, if she sat here holding it one more second, he would know that she had this problem about bodywaste disposal. She wadded the mess decisively into her pocket, next to Illogical Fears. He was still jotting.

"Also bites cuticles," he had written. "Somewhat short-waisted? Call Lesley *Re* Sat. nite."

Altogether she blew 270 hours, 9,450 dollars and possibly an even thousand Kleenex on him. He never once said he loved her, or invited her for the slightest peek behind the other door to see whether he lived back there—and if so, how. Once she nearly asked to use his bathroom; legally there had to be a bathroom, like in restaurants, she thought. But then she remembered how Dorothy in *The Wizard of Oz* forcefully pried open the curtain to expose the Wizard's true identity. Like Oz, she would find Dr. S. Conrad Foxx to be an ordinary Henry Morgan of a man with wire hangers in his suits and chipped tiles above his tub. He would have iceberg lettuce wilting in a refrigerator that needed cleaning. A curly hair or two would nestle in his sink; gray dust would be gathering in soft balls under his unmade bed, and he would be incapable of sending her back home to

Kansas, even if that was what she wanted most in the world.

So she wisely never asked to use his bathroom.

Toward the end she did tell him a few of the better fantasies. Including the internal examination by twenty-five academically outstanding members of a well-known college fraternity, later suspended for their part in the alleged incident. "Look at that one her, will you?" one of them says. "Hey, did you get a load of *this?*"

Also the Lexington Avenue subway dream in which the man in the filthy raincoat lurches over and clamps his black-gloved fingers over her hand, on the overhead bar. "The train careens into 51st Street, and he leads me out, up the stairs, into the men's toilet. He orders me to undress, and then flings my clothes into a nasty wet puddle. Perverts are loitering in adjacent cubicles. Their trousers are all bunched suspiciously around their ankles. They come out to stare at us, pointing with their . . . but suddenly the raincoat man backs away. 'What is it?' I cry. 'What's *wrong?*'

" 'Nothing,' he snarls. 'Only I didn't expect . . . *that.*' He points. 'Or that, either.'

"I begin to cry; I say I'm sorry. I keep trying to cover myself, but all my clothes are in these nasty wet puddles, and the toilet-paper dispensers are empty. 'Wait up,' I call. But he's gone. Even the perverts are gone. I can still hear them outside, zipping their flies."

In her secret world, the wages of sin always turned out to be well below the standard minimum.

Then one day she abruptly announced that she was quitting. "I'm leaving you," she said. He didn't seem surprised. Now don't expect him to seem surprised, she had warned herself sternly. Didn't Freud say there was no such thing as surprises? Actually, what Freud said was that there was no such thing as jokes, and anyway, Dr. Foxx was not a Freudian. If he had been a Freudian, wouldn't he have charged her when she missed two hours because of the intestinal flu virus? Would he have smiled when she said something funny? He most certainly would, and would not, respectively. Furthermore, he would have sat there in grim silence accusing her of once believing her own mother had a penis, or of wishing she had one herself to *give* to her mother. Happy Mother's Day! If Freud wasn't into jokes, he certainly must have been crazier than she was. She would also bet that Freud had never let anyone look in his bathroom (where he kept all that cocaine). Except maybe Anna.

Aloud she only asked Dr. Foxx, "Don't *you* think I'm well enough to quit therapy?"

"Don't *you?*" he countered. She should have expected that too. Damn him, she thought, swallowing hard. She would not, she had vowed, dampen one more Kleenex from his rotten box. She would sit silently for the next ten minutes, willing him to beg her not to go.

"Oh, please," she imagined he would whisper, with the soft silky voice of Dorian Gray seducing the first of his thousand victims. That little fool of a tavern singer! She would stay with him all night

18

because he asked. She would kill herself first thing in the morning because she stayed.

S. Conrad Foxx did not ask. He sighed, glancing at his watch, and said that unfortunately her hour was up. He said his door would remain open, however, in case she felt she ever needed . . . She knew he did not mean the *other* door, the one leading into his life and/or bathroom.

Whether he had helped her was now just one more thing she really couldn't say. Although on the way out that last time, if she'd had to venture an opinion, she would have ventured Yes, but only because she still believed it was generally nicer to say yes to people if you possibly could without feeling dishonest.

The fact was, she would still opt for the sexual fantasy over the genuine act, any time. Hands down. So far her phantom United Parcel man had never drawn blood. So far Burton F. Bigelow, twisted sodomizer and self-confessed slayer of coed hitchhikers in the greater Cleveland area (they asked for it; they hopped right in, didn't they?), had merely forced her imagination to perform to the unbearable strain of Beethoven's 4th or 5th. Whereas an actual living self-supporting penis, even that of a nice person from a Crisis Intervention Center, *hurt*. For a total of $9,450, S. Conrad Foxx, M.D., had not been of much help about that. Although he *had* pointed out why it was all her fault.

The pain, she had learned, even the bleeding, was nothing more than an overt act of sheer hostility on her part. Stop hating, stop hurting. SH, SH—it had a certain catchiness to it. She certainly intended to try it out on the Crisis Intervention man. Harry was his name. Stop Hating Harry, Stop Harry Hurting. SHH, SHH.

Why, with any luck at all, she might even find true orgasm with Harry. True orgasm was something Dr. Foxx recommended very highly. It would beat anything she had ever had with any fantasy, he could guarantee that. She wondered if he had any idea what nice orgasms she had with the fantasies about him. Ah, *those*, he would say, not unkindly. Those, I'm afraid, are merely more of your little clitoral things, that's all *those* are. Shoddy goods, suitable for girls who don't have their full growth on them, and maybe neurotics who never will. Second-fiddlers. But the adult female, what she gets is your true orgasm. That would be your vaginal model, available only through authorized dealers. Nothing whatever like *those*. Dr. Foxx would shrug. Nothing whatever.

But true orgasm still lay shimmering somewhere beyond SH, SH: beyond fantasy, beyond the clitoris, beyond her wildest childest orgiastic dreams. The big vaginal O at the tail end of poor Dorothy's rainbow. Oz had spoken.

On the other hand, as Dr. Foxx himself had noted with cautious optimism on the last page of the spiral notebook pertaining to her case: "Cuticles appear intact. May have stopped biting."

In the larger sense, Dr. Foxx must have known perfectly well that she had not stopped biting, and it must have mattered to him more than he could admit in a spiral notebook. Because two years later, right after her amicable divorce from Harry, S. Conrad Foxx suddenly called up to just say hello and how she was getting on, and then came right over, making his first house call, and then took her to bed, or rather, to the living-room carpet, with the kissing exactly the way she always imagined, but the touching too quick and rough and silent, and then when it all stopped as suddenly as if his entire body had glanced at his watch and indicated that he was, ah, running a little late, the first thing she thought of was asking him for a full refund.

He would have laughed, she bet. He still had that nice low kind of self-conscious erupting laugh that he used to give her like an allowance when she said something funny that caught him off guard. Then he would cut it off sharply the minute he noticed something fishy about what she hadn't said that he should have been analyzing. "You on the pill?" he demanded now, sharply.

"Uh, no. No. In fact, I'm totally *against* the pill. You know, because of the thrombo-whatever it is known to cause." It was good the room was so dark; he would never catch her avoiding his frown.

"You're not wearing a diaphragm."

"Oh, that. Yes, well, *that* was broken," she said quickly. Guilty with a highly unlikely explanation. "I sort of let it expire last June, along with my driver's license."

He was going to disapprove of her. She recognized the silence, even with his arms around her.

"I really didn't think I'd be needing them," she went on, faster and one tone higher, hoping he wouldn't remember the sound of impending tears in her voice. "Since Harry did all the driving and we only had oral-genital contact the last year."

"Harry," he noted dryly, "doesn't live here any more."

"I'm sorry," she apologized. If he asked what for, she would have to think of something. Maybe he would forget to ask. Maybe he would forget the whole thing and just hold her. Maybe the hour wouldn't be up.

It was, though. "Crazy," he mumbled nervously, feeling around her for his underwear. He had to, uh, get home; he had a seven A.M. patient. God knows how he would find a parking space at this hour. He kept stepping over her scattered limbs in search of his other sock. She lay there on the red high-pile carpet like a carelessly dropped toy. Still a crazy person, she thought, picking a crazy doctor. Then she smiled bravely to herself, reaching down to touch herself, drawing her thighs to a slippery close.

"You'll catch cold lying there like that," he said.

"Oh," she answered, rolling over on her stomach. "Better?"

"Poor baby." He knelt, Dr. Foxx *knelt*, beside her for an instant and touched her all the way down her back with warm fingertips. She shivered. "You're beautiful naked," he whispered softly. "I used to think a little short-waisted."

"Nevertheless!" she screamed, having kept this big lump waiting in her throat until he had shut her front door and gone down in the elevator. "Nevertheless," she sobbed, "since in your own words I am every bit as crazy as the first time I saw you, the fact remains I am entitled to a refund *in full!*"

Then she licked the tears carefully from around her smile. Crazy, she thought, like a Foxx. She would show him crazy. Dear Department of Consumer Affairs—that's right, of Consumer Haha *Affairs*—I would like to report, in the interest of a possible 9,450 dollars back . . .

After a while she stopped crying and began to stroke herself slowly. Whispering, "By the way, Doctor, what do you think of this? Or of this, for that matter?" In the fantasy she came to him naked while he jotted things down in his note pad about what she wanted him to touch, and how, and now over here a little. Mm, yes, ah. In the fantasy he would come as she pleased, and so would she. It was just the way she had always wanted it. Until now.

But when he called her the next morning at 7:08 (his patient was late), his voice sounded so inexplicably tender that she decided not to report him after all, because who could possibly file a deposition against a voice like that?

He called twice more that day, for no discernible reason, so that at 7:08 the *next* morning she woke up needing the sound of that hello of his. He must have known this, though neither of them said so. The thought that he might also have some need never occurred to either of them.

He told himself that he was making up, in a way, for failing her the last time. Also, he told himself, she really *was* beautiful naked. Especially for a nut.

Chapter

TWO

THE MEETING NEVER came to order, which of course was one of its endearing features. They should have started an hour ago, but then Joanne telephoned to say she was rehearsing late, and Margot hadn't bothered to call at all, so even if she was coming, they no longer expected her. They were into the second bottle of California burgundy, the ashtrays were full of take-out fried-chicken bones, what was left of the Brie looked like an embarrassing infection, and they had spent the last forty minutes exhausting all the possible hidden reasons why Joanne wasn't coming tonight, and why Margot never called, and whether anyone else was sick of take-out fried chicken.

She couldn't possibly explain what it was about this group that delighted her so. Why she should feel such a leap of excitement before every meeting, when she couldn't remember anything that happened last time, not even who was there or what the topic was. Sexual Boredom in Marriage again, probably.

Basically, what did they do besides gather together for the pure gathering together of it? She could not have said. Knotting and painfully retying little threads of themselves, like Victorian ladies embroidering the first clumsy sampler: There is so much Good in the Worst of Us/And so much Bad in the Best of Us/That it ill behooves Any of Us/To talk about the Rest of Us. Entwined in a border of forget-me-knots, with interesting double-crossed loyalties and tiny shocking intimacies woven in at random to balance the pattern.

Presumably they were joined together here, the five or six or eight of them, for serious political purposes. Charting the slow rising of female consciousness like some new, disputed constellation shrouded by natural nebulae or husbands or ordinary passing clouds. Presumably they came to cry, and to stare at their own reflections in each other's tears. Hugging like children waking from identical nightmares, and offering reckless confidences in exchange for "You too?" Roach-infested kitchens, they confessed; chronic guilt for having children, or not having; gagging with a cock in the mouth; writer's block; painter's block; orgasm block; stumbling . . .

Never mind, she was madly in love with it. She

26

soaked in the ritual like a convert in her spiritual
bubble bath, radiant with mystic faith. "This *women's*
group," she would say of it tremulously, "this *group*
I belong to."

Something like school, yes, she would say. Something like sophomoric. Except that in school she had
been positive they were all philosophers, all plumb-
ing mysterious universal truths. The morality of
suicide before graduation, assuming one has never
published one's poems. The question of whether a
man who uses the word love while making it is any
more loving, really, than one who only uses it before-
hand. And would any man ever use it *after?* To *me?*
How many angels would even consider dancing on
the head of a penis?

In school nobody had to find out anything for
sure. Womanhood seemed beautiful from afar. There
was no wine or Brie or chicken, only fifty-cent bags
of powdery oozing jelly doughnuts that must have
been symbols of their sexual selves, if only they had
noticed. Fulfillment lay just beyond the next bite,
when you got to the jelly center; achievement lay in
never breaking out from it. She remembered them
all perfectly: Claire, who underwent electrolysis of
the thighs for the sake of a two-piece bathing suit;
Gladys, who was a technical virgin; Vicky, who wore
three strategic drops of L'Air du Temps to bed every
night, regardless; Betsy, who had a heavy monthly
flow; Anita, who had excessive oiliness and black-
heads which she squeezed in front of them, exclaim-
ing "Gotcha!" All of them sharing the same secret

dread that their bodies would always be like this
... this *ugly*, but no one ever saying it.

College was different because they had known
that someday they would graduate. It had taken her
twelve years to move from that group of girls to this
one of women, only to discover that she had never
graduated at all.

She discovered it the night her voice changed.
Suddenly in the middle of her turn to speak she
noticed this lustrous quality to it, a melodic rise and
fall. Forceful was how it sounded. Magnetic. Usually
she spoke in a low-pitched monotone, suitable for
the public library, where it says SILENCE. People
either never quite heard her, and didn't care, or
kept saying "What?" or nodded as if they *had* heard,
and moved on quickly to someone less . . . well, *boring*. Which was fine, really, because she knew that if
they actually paid careful attention to her, she would
have to stand there slowly strangling in her own
voice, watching these people, whoever they were,
stifling their yawns. She would be imprisoned in
their glazed eyes, locked in their frozen smiles—and
they would all die before her sentence ended.

So when she heard this funny change, this dis-
tinctly vibrant sound coming out of her throat, making
such excellent hilarious sense that everyone in the
room immediately understood, and laughed or gasped
or nodded vigorously in all the right places, she
stopped talking even though it was still her turn,
and stared incredulously around her. No one said
anything; they just sat there waiting for her to go

on. Waiting for the rest of her shimmering, modulated thought to cast tiny sparks of rainbowed light across the room like one of those big round globes covered with little squares of mirror that used to twirl slowly overhead in the gym on the night of the prom she hadn't been asked to. The voice was—she was—dazzling.

"Hey," she exclaimed softly. "Hey, listen to me." The other women of the group smiled uncertainly at her. The other women—this odd mix of strangers who would probably never be real friends, who had husbands or analysts or children or jobs or parties on all their other nights. She didn't want to share the rest of their lives at all, nor they hers. But even their uncertain smiles warmed her. She bit thoughtfully into another fried-chicken leg.

"What's tonight's topic, anyway?" Tess asked irritably. Tess had to leave early tonight; she was having her intrauterine device removed tomorrow.

"Fear of success?" Wanda suggested. Wanda had been depressed since her last recital, which the *Village Voice* dance critic had called "luminous and haunting."

"Sexual boredom in marriage," said Sophy firmly.

"I'd like to . . . I mean, I have a specific problem," she volunteered. They were silent at once. "Last night," she began. "I slept with my analyst last night." *Screwed,* she had meant to say. Not slept with. And *former* analyst. She still had this impulse to dramatize. Playing for the reverent hush, the sharp intake of breath. You *did?* You actually *did?* "Former analyst," she amended.

Still, there was a fair amount of thoughtful silence. Munching of cracker crumbs. More wine hastily poured.

Then what was the problem, Laurie asked finally. "*Former* analyst screwing *former* patient," she pointed out, wasn't an exploitive situation. "I mean *per se*, anyway," she added, not to seem unsympathetic. Laurie was very big on exploitation, *per se*.

"The problem, Laurie," she replied quietly, "is that the whole time I was in therapy he never told me one single thing that was true, and now I need him worse than ever."

"What for?" Wanda asked.

She hesitated as long as possible. Then she shrugged. "I guess love." Now she felt really embarrassed. Almost nothing she had ever told them embarrassed her like this—though she had told them things she had never dreamed of telling Dr. Foxx. "If he loved me," she said, "if my *analyst* loved me, my analyst who knows more about me than I could even tell him if I wanted to, let alone my husband . . . I mean, if my analyst *loved* me, it would prove I'm okay. As a woman. It would prove—"

"Bullshit," Laurie exploded. "It would prove you should have gone to a woman analyst."

"Well," she sighed, "maybe I would now. Except to me it's still like looking at yourself in a mirror. Or at your mother. The mirror never shows you how a *man* sees you."

"Bull*shit!*" Laurie again. "Who cares how a man sees you? Why don't you care how you *are?*"

"I don't know, Laurie." She really didn't; she felt very tired suddenly. "Someone else's turn," she said. God, she wished she hadn't told them.

Chapter

THREE

Dr. foxx had not seen his license or registration since he left her house Sunday night. They must have dropped out of his pants pocket. He couldn't find his wallet either, but chances were he hadn't lost that there. In fact, he couldn't remember having the wallet since Thursday. But the other stuff, he was positive. He had been calling her three times a day to see if she'd found anything. Damn her. Screwing on the floor like high school kids. He should have known she'd pull a stunt like that. "Not in Harry's bed." For Crissake.

She had taken her place apart for him. She had picked up that whole living-room rug by herself; she had picked through her garbage; she had even gone down to poke around the incinerator room. He had this horrified flash of her charred remains being shoveled out of there, with his license and registration clutched in her hot little self-destructive fist.

It served him right, he knew. Screwing around with a patient. *Former* patient, all right, but you don't get off on a technicality in this business. The principle still applied, he would be the first to say, if he heard it about anyone else. If he had to bet his life on it, he couldn't think of one other analyst who'd ever screwed around with a patient. Not even a former.

Maybe he had left the wallet in his glove compartment Thursday? He raced out into the cold, shirt sleeves flapping, just as his next patient rounded the corner. "Hi, Dr. Foxx," the boy said, checking his watch.

"Oh, hello, Clyde, right with you." Mustering a dignified frown. Good thing he wasn't a Freudian; he'd have died trying to maintain unreality. Harry Stack Sullivan, on the other hand, used to take patients walking in the park. No reason why a Sullivanian in perfectly good standing couldn't be seen running toward his car in the snow, wearing only a short-sleeved shirt. No reason at all, he told himself sternly, except that you look like a nut.

There was nothing in the glove compartment except a button from his raincoat, two halves of a Dexedrine tablet—better take one of those right now, matter of fact—and a bunch of torn scraps of paper on which he had scrawled, at one time or another over the past six months: "On Urgent Medical Call, 225 East 16th Street, Bergman"; "On Urgent Medical Call, 325 Park Avenue, Morrison"; "On Urgent Medical Call, 125 West 58th Street, McDonough." Names and addresses of women he had dated since last July. Have to throw those away sometime, he thought.

Could he have worn *brown* pants, Sunday?

Clyde was one of the few patients he had who still used the couch. Dr. Foxx kept a sheet of plastic on one end for the feet, and a plastic-covered wedge pillow on the other end for the head. The plastic on both ends was grimy, and crackled when touched, which might explain why few patients other than Clyde used the couch any more.

Clyde's problem was that he couldn't get it up with his wife. Any other woman, no sweat. Used to be no sweat with his wife either, until they got married. Virtually a classic case, Clyde. Make a nice paper for "Medical Aspects of Human Sexuality," if he ever got around to it. "Characteristic Sexual Dysfunction in Marriage as an Inevitable Concomitant . . ." But he really couldn't handle that right now. The instant Clyde left he picked up the phone and called her. "Hi!" she said breathlessly. She had just finished searching the elevator shaft, from underneath.

"I only called to see how you were," he said stiffly.

She was roasting this lamb, she said. He *was* coming for dinner, wasn't he?

In his own refrigerator he had two limp carrots and a solidly frozen tuna pie, plus the last of six little turkey sandwiches he had thoughtfully saved from the collation following last week's meeting at the Institute. Five days old today, that little turkey sandwich. "Uh, no," he declared firmly. "I said I'd be busy tonight."

"Working?"

"Busy."

"Well, if it's work, you could go right back after you eat. I *swear*. I already put it in, the lamb."

"Well." No. "Maybe tomorrow." He could feel her not breathing. "By the way, you didn't happen to find—"

"No." Pause. Last chance. "*Please* come tonight." She bit her lip. She apologized for having this hunger to feed him. She would gladly roast herself instead for not having found his license and registration. Basting occasionally. Maybe then he would let her feed him.

"Well . . ."

Obviously, there was no need to roast herself. Any psychiatrist could have told her that, and in his own way, Dr. Foxx did try to tell her. At first.

At first he simply said no. Please don't. I don't need, I don't want. But she always insisted. And he always gave in, or so it seemed. He would come just to let her feed him. Or make love. The briefest, most noncommittal love. Somehow he began to end up there every night, still protesting No; *really*, not tonight. And then he would lose his keys there, or his appointment book, or all the notes for his paper on "Clinically Significant Depression," which she had offered to type for him while he went to Long Island for the weekend without her.

Nights that he didn't come, she spent searching for his things—the keys or the papers or the top button on the new blue shirt she had bought him. Without the top button he wouldn't be able to wear the shirt tomorrow, regardless of the fact that she had stood there last night sprinkling it with her tears before ironing it so that he could wear it to this party he was going to with someone else.

There was no need whatever to roast herself, but she needed to just the same. And after six months this need of hers infuriated him almost as much as his willingness to indulge it.

Still he would come, hating himself, and let her do what she had to—up to a point. Then he would pile his books and papers beside the bed like protective sandbags for the undeclared war between them. He would climb into her bed and fasten his eyes to a page of print, any page, regardless of the hour, so as not to need to look at her needing him to look at her. And they would lie apart like any decently married couple keeping up appearances for the children's sake.

Or she would slip down under the covers and touch him with her fingers or her mouth until he snapped at her to stop it because he was trying— couldn't she see?—to work and wouldn't she ever once consider *his* needs instead of her own for a change. He would be reading last month's *Psychiatric Spectator*.

"But you're only reading last month's *Psychiatric*

Spectator!" she would point out, which was always a mistake.

"So what?" he would thunder. "I'm getting *ready* to work."

It would be one-thirty in the morning, but by then she would know better than to point this out. "I want," she would say softly instead, "to make love now."

"Never think of anyone but yourself!" he would shout. "Never occur to you that *I*—"

And the next night he would not come at all.

So after a while she learned to turn her back to him in time, so that he would not see either her tears or her solution. Which was to lie next to him, not quite touching, and tell herself this story about how he'd come to spend the night and just change the ending ever so slightly. She would tell it so that this time Dr. Foxx would be here naked in her bed, ignoring her like this, eyes fastened just so on his *Psychiatric Spectator*, and she would lie beside him in solitary sexy agony, only without any covers on, so that out of the corner of his fastened eye he would have to see what she was doing. "Please," he would groan finally, hurling the magazine across the room. "Please . . . let *me*."

"Are you crying?" he asked uncomfortably, when she had lain quietly a little too long.

"No," she said. Very composed.

"Well, what *are* you doing?"

"I'm working," she said. "Like you."

Dr. Foxx groaned and popped half of something into his mouth. He always took only half.

"Is that a waking-up half, or a sleeping?" she asked. "I just want to know what mood to assume."

He laughed at that. The first present he had given her all night. "I love you," she murmured, breaking the solemn promise not to say that today, on pain of . . . Then she curled herself tightly away from him. Now where was she in the dream . . .

He groaned again, and turned off the light, and reached around her to cover her breasts with his hands, like a child playing Guess Who. Fitting the curved front of him snugly to the curved back of her, as if they were to be put away neatly together in the drawer with the good silver.

He always fell asleep like that. First.

Of course there were times he surprised them both. Once he called and said, "Hey, come meet me." Just like that. And she walked to him through the night streets; four miles, she walked, as if on hot coals, like a human sacrifice. She found him standing outside the restaurant, his eyes searching for her in the darkness. "Hi," he said to her softly, instead of scolding her for walking alone that way through the streets, like a nut. And she stared at him, standing there under the street light; it was so strange that he should be anywhere at all, waiting for her. He was wearing a white dinner jacket and looked like a parody of some portrait in his high school yearbook.

He wanted to go to this restaurant, he explained, because there was a dance band that reminded him of when he was a kid dating girls. She wouldn't eat, of course; that was one of the nutty things she did with him, not eat. And he would not urge her to, or even ask why; that was one of the other nutty things. Anyway, they danced to the dance band's old slow music that reminded him of when he was a kid dating girls. They danced together clinging, but saying nothing.

Then he didn't call her for a week.

It was Margot who suggested that the whole group punch Dr. Foxx in the nose. At one time or another, Margot had suggested nose-punching for the husbands or lovers of nearly every member of the group. Not for her own, though. Nowadays Margot consorted only with known homosexuals, and whatever they needed from her, punching was presumably not it.

Tess kept talking about the *symbiosis* of it. Dr. Foxx was not being exploitive, didn't they get it? He was terrified of love, was all.

"He's a sadist, is all," snapped Margot.

"Of course he's a sadist; I'm trying to explain *why* he's a sadist," Tess retorted. "Jesus!"

"Fuck him!" Laurie exploded finally. "What are we analyzing *him* for? What about *her*? I mean, here's this person who used to talk about being a serious writer, for instance. Then she turns into a serious *masochist*. And all *we* do is sit around worrying about some nut named Dr. Foxx! What about her *work*, damn it? What about—"

"Oh, Laurie," sighed Wanda. "Who cares about work when their love life stinks?"

"*Men* do," said Tess. "Doris Lessing said she

never met a man who'd fuck up his work for a love affair, and she never met a woman who wouldn't."

"Doris Lessing never said 'fuck up,'" replied Wanda, "but that's a terriffc topic for next week."

"Next week?" she wailed. "What about in the meantime? What about how Dr. Foxx won't even *touch* me any more?"

"He won't?" said Sophy with renewed interest. "What happens in bed?"

"He *reads* in bed!" she sobbed. "I lie there quivering under his pile of *Psychiatric Spectators,* and I'm the only issue he never gets to!"

"Sexual boredom strikes again," murmured Sophy.

"Maybe he needs the message in writing," said Tess.

"Yeah, maybe," said Laurie, "if she could find a way to come weekly, in a plain brown wrapper."

The following week she came to the meeting dressed as a sex object: silver miniskirt, see-through halter, black lipstick and three-inch platform shoes with ankle straps. She almost broke her leg climbing the stairs to Wanda's loft.

"Tonight's topic," she announced, removing her coat, "is soft-core porn. Exhibit A."

Dr. Foxx had taken her to this cocktail party, dumped her, and gone to say hello to an old friend. She had gulped three drinks at the bar, on top of her sixty mg of Dexamyl, and passed out. When she came to, still on the bar stool, three strange men were conducting independent probes of her condition, and Dr. Foxx was across the room with the old friend, observing.

"He's terrified of love," said Laurie dryly.

Tess said nothing.

"A punch," muttered Margot, "in the nose."

Chapter

FOUR

HE SAT WATCHING Sunday disappear behind
two scrubby Long Island trees. Shivering slightly,
he would nevertheless finish reading at least the
sports section before going in. Going in meant ac-
knowledging that the weekend was over, the solitary
peace of it all used up. She had spent the two days
waiting for him to come back. She had done his
laundry and retyped the mess of a paper he left for
her to proofread for him, and now she was making
dinner. He couldn't stop her; he had set her in motion
and now she was scrabbling up this infinite mountain of his dumb needs because she had to. Of *course*
he minded, of *course* he felt the guilt, but that was
only another mountain. He had no right to take

this . . . love of hers, as she insisted on calling it. Guilty as hell, your honor, but how much happier would she be if I said no? Think about it.

She had already called to find out what time he was coming back. He knew she had sat there for two days waiting until it was all right to call and ask him that. Seven o'clock? he had said wearily. Eight? Whenever, she had forced herself to say. It was nearly eight now, and he'd be at least another two hours, with traffic, even if he left at once. And there was still the News of the Week section, and the Book Review, and the last golden shards of the sunset. Damn her. He could see her ten-o'clock face confronting him. No reproach, not a word, just the little flicker of bottomless hurt in her eyes—her version of the Eternal Flame. She would never understand that he was fighting her for his life. Traffic, he would say uncomfortably. I got a late start. I had to clear up some . . . things.

He started to dial her number. No, better not. Maybe she'd break the pattern, yell at him just this once. You bastard! Two hours late! Maybe she'd give up and slam the door and go to a movie. Screw him! Let him get a hamburger. Let him eat cake. Or shit. He smiled. Not a chance. Not her.

He still remembered how she was on that first day when she walked into his office. Such a sad girl, he had thought. Wishing she hadn't come to *him* for help, not then, when he couldn't possibly . . . She was the first private patient he'd ever had. He'd do better by her now. If only she were his patient now, instead of his . . . whatever she was.

She surprised him, though. She wasn't there. She left him a cooked pot roast, and his clean laundry, and his paper on "Depression," neatly typed, and a long letter, fifteen handwritten pages stapled together. It was addressed "To Dr. Foxx. Something to read in bed. My Turn."

She was going away for a while, she said. She didn't say where, but she did say "I love you." The rest of the letter, she said, would speak for itself.

The pot roast was delicious, though his grandmother would have remembered to put a little white horseradish on the side. His grandmother would have loaded it on his plate, saying, "Eat, my Sandor, *eletem*. You are my whole life." And his stepfather would have made him gag on the first bite. He could hear his stepfather's voice thundering, "Pig! Did you see that? He took the best piece! I want him served *last* from now on. *Last!* Is that clear?"

Dr. Foxx put the fork down. Suddenly he wasn't so hungry for pot roast.

TO DR. FOXX. UTTERLY CONFIDENTIAL

MY TURN

TOPIC: FATNESS

I used to be very fat. I mean really fat. When I was about 16 I weighed 172 one day, and I threw the scale into the closet with my pile of dirty underpants.

I hated: boys who were handsome; girls who were thin; belts; my mother, who was thin; waist cinchers; my nose; my hair; panty girdles that pushed you up;

lastex bathing suits that pushed you down; nice clothes; parties. Not necessarily in that order, but close.

The reason I hated all those things was that they didn't fit together in any constructive way for me. Everyone else seemed to have a body and face and clothes and a boy or boys who took them to parties or saw them in bathing suits. It all went together like a matching set of real coral jewelry. Even the mothers of other girls were either fatter than the girls were or else imperfect in other noticeable ways, so that they couldn't afford to pick on their daughters for not measuring up or down.

As soon as I was old enough to skip dessert I bought a long mauve organdy dress two sizes too small and began taking nightly enemas. I also bought strange shoes that I thought were sexy. I sort of liked my ankles. One pair of shoes I bought had three-inch heels and long black velvet ribbons that were supposed to wind up around your ankles like gladiator sandals. The shoes themselves were pink silk with little white dots. They cost $45, and I never wore them. I kept them in the box for 6 years.

Somehow I met a handsome boy around that time, and somehow he liked me. I went to a dance with him in this mauve organdy dress that was still too small in spite of the enemas, and he thought I looked pretty, he said, not having noticed that the seams were straining something fierce across the midriff. I mean the midriff of the dress. The word is commonly used to describe that portion of the body between the waist and the bosom. At the time my waist was 30 inches, and my bosom 34 (A cup). I do not consider that I have ever personally had a midriff of my own. But this boy who liked me was not aware that I had no midriff. Perhaps he was too dumb to spot it. Also, I don't think he was aware of how handsome he was; otherwise he would very definitely have had a girl whose looks conformed somewhat more closely to at least the national average.

I don't really know how this boy felt about my body because though he liked touching it here and there, I was always twisting it around and sucking it in just in case he happened to touch any other places accidentally. I used to hold my breath during heavy petting, which made it difficult to control what he touched, at least by word of mouth.

He was the first person ever to insert a fingertip in any orifice of mine. I had never until then believed I actually had an orifice that would be of any use to anyone. I certainly did not think I had one of a size suitable for insertion of anything, not even a Junior Tampax, much less a sophomore cock.

By the time we drifted apart, this dumb Adonis and I, he had put a finger all the way up inside me, and I had held his entire cock in my hand, and I was more firmly convinced than ever that nothing like that would ever make it where his finger had gone. He ejaculated once onto a plaid skirt I had, and said he wanted to save himself for our wedding night. As I recall, I said I was glad, but I don't think I really was.

About a century later, when I was 19, I discovered a steak and lettuce diet and went on it for two years. I also discovered, probably not as a direct result of the diet, but simultaneously, that I could masturbate to orgasm, which would, as I saw it, eliminate once and for all the necessity of any man's ever seeing or touching any of the fat or ugly parts.

In retrospect I would say that the worst thing about ever having been fat and ugly is that it is an incur-

able mental *condition. I weigh 109 pounds now and wear a size 7, and yet I think constantly about how I look to Dr. Foxx and whether some part of me really feels all right to his touch.*

Last week I went to a party wearing a see-through crochet dress over a body stocking, so that I appeared practically naked from three feet away. I saw this naked body reflected in the eyes of every man there. What I felt was that it was not me they were looking at, but some naked foreign body I happened to have on under the crochet dress. What I truly felt was that I had borrowed the entire rig for the evening. Dr. Foxx stood next to me and smiled whenever any other man stared at me. What I felt about that was that he was really proud of my attachments, as if somehow he was wearing them too.

TOPIC: SEXINESS

Last weekend I was on the beach at Stone's Throw Island and he was on the beach at Laconic Bay, and I called him and he said you can't get here from there. It would take you, he said, an hour on the ferry and another hour on the bus, and the bus would only stop at some gas station on Montauk Highway and I am entirely too busy to drive to any gas station in order to pick you up, because I have a tennis game then. Whenever it is.

So I called up a seaplane service and said I will be wearing this white bikini and carrying only a small straw bag, and you can pick me up on the beach here right away, and take me to the beach there, and I don't care what it costs.

So the seaplane dipped down into the bay off Stone's Throw Island and I climbed aboard, in my white bikini, and waved my straw bag at the gleaming volleyball-playing Stone's Throw Island men who waved back even though the sun was in their eyes, and 10 minutes to the day later the seaplane dipped down into the bay off Laconic Point, docking approximately two yards from the tennis court where he was playing, and I stepped lightly out and paid the pilot handsomely, 52 dollars and change, to be exact. Everyone at this tennis club was buzzing around, gasping in wonderment and admiration at this dazzling girl in the white bikini stepping out of this silver seaplane. No one before or since had ever pulled such a stunt. He did not even bother to come off the court to say hello, because, as he later explained, it was set point in the club tournament.

I didn't cry much, and I guess that pleased him, because he was very loving the whole rest of the weekend. That night, when I went down on him in bed, he stroked my hair and said, God, you're great, you really like doing that, don't you?

That wasn't where the sexiness came in, though, you understand. For me, the sexiness was when I came down to him out of the sky, like in a song or a movie musical, and he wouldn't even come off the tennis court to say hello.

TOPIC: FANTASIES

The fact is that I have never had a rape fantasy. I think that's what men have. What I have are fantasies about men giving me orders to do an interesting assortment of other things, including masturbating in public or walking around naked on all fours in front of them, so that they can jeer at whatever sags or droops or otherwise seems entertaining.

In all my fantasies the men are nasty, fully dressed and faintly amused. I am always silent, nude, obedient and, most of all, ludicrous. But I am never raped. I am never pinned down, violently stripped, beaten up or overpowered. I am never subjected to brute force. I never struggle.

One fantasy I have features this surly husband with what appears to be a two-day growth of beard, who orders me to masturbate at the breakfast table while he reads the paper and crunches his toast. This image is undoubtedly based on a lifetime of seeing cartoons that show a married couple at the breakfast table. The wife is invariably angry because her husband pays no attention to her. The husband is invariably cowering behind his paper because the wife is wearing jumbo hair rollers and face cream and yapping at him about not looking at her—which, of course, he can't bear to do. So they sulk on opposite sides of this insurmountable daily-paper wall (that he erects). There is always a steaming coffeepot on the table, and a plate of eggs and toast (in front of him,), and this homey universal truth that people who are married must acquire a lifelong habit of avoiding each other's most fundamental needs first thing in the morning, so that they won't forget to hate each other the rest of the day.

Another fantasy I have involves the editor of a magazine I once worked for. He is a suave, aggressive type who smokes little cigars and keeps his desk top neat and empty. It is a huge, dark, gleaming rosewood slab of a desk top—two or three phones bristling with buttons, dictating machines, a typical big-shot desk. In the fantasy I am his secretary (I have never been a secretary), but I have to wear a little French maid's ruffled white pinafore and a little

*cap. Nothing else, except a pencil behind my ear and
a steno pad in my little ruffled pocket. When he
buzzes for me, I come in and he barks "Come here."
Then, "Unbutton that and give me those. First the
left one."*

*Then he tells me to bend over, with my back to
him. I am to stand there, not moving, just bend over
like that, with my apron ruffling out and this perky
bow over my rear end, while he answers his tele-
phones, dictates memos and opens his mail. Every so
often he reaches over and fondles some portion of me.
It appears to help him concentrate on his work, like
scratching one's ear or chewing pencils. Occasionally
he snaps his fingers or signals me to assume another
position. He never consummates the relationship; in
fact, he never moves out of the chair. I see only his
head and the top of his body—the white shirt, tie and
conservative navy-blue suit. Sexually, I find the whole
scene almost unbearably exciting.*

*I can think of only one fantasy involving actual in-
tercourse, and though it seems as masochistic as the
others, it is the only one in which I appear to be the
aggressor.*

*Dr. Foxx is seated in his office chair (why are the
men always sitting down?) and I come in for my
analytic hour. He doesn't bother to look up, merely
nods vaguely and motions me toward my customary
seat. He is obviously preoccupied. (That's another
thing about the men in my fantasies: they're always
preoccupied.) I begin to take off my clothes, and I
note that he is jotting this down. I start to walk slowly
toward him. I am not trying to be seductive, but I am
definitely coming over to have sex with him, and he
seems to know this. Finally he stops taking notes and
helps me arrange myself so that we can screw. He*

remains composed (and fully dressed); only I move. After a while I ask him to do certain things with his hands or mouth. Mostly I want him to touch my breasts and kiss them. He does so.

Outside his window a policeman walks past, looks in and winks slyly. Man to man. Dr. Foxx winks back and shrugs, expressing helpless embarrassment, as if to explain to the policeman that even a psychiatrist has to endure this kind of thing at times. The policeman winks again and moves on, whistling.

I frequently use this fantasy to masturbate to when I am in bed with Dr. Foxx.

TOPIC: LOVE

I've never wanted anything as hard as I want Dr. Foxx. I say I "love" him, but there ought to be another name for it. Fixation, maybe. Foxxation.

Anyway, it's nothing like romantic. Love—a lover —means somebody tender, impulsively buying violets for your furs because they match your eyes and the spring in his heart. Somebody thinking you're beautiful even with your glasses or clothes on. Your ugliest clothes. Robert Young and Dorothy McGuire in The Enchanted Cottage. *We can see that they're both horribly disfigured, but all they see is Dorothy Mc-Guire and Robert Young. Perfect.*

I've known a few tender men. They always made me uncomfortable. Violets? To match my eyes? Oh, come on. What would I want with a man who couldn't see me clearly, warts and all? And call them warts. But tenderly.

So I hurl myself against Stonewall Foxx, this man who wouldn't dream of giving me violets. And while I'm hurling, I'm dreaming violets, violets. Someday he's got to lay them on me, I just know it. It isn't the dream I'm hooked on; it's the impossibility. It will never happen. Even if that kind of love is possible, I'm making it impossible. In Dr. Foxx's garden of earthly delights, believe me, there are no violets.

So I guess he is my ideal lover. He gives me what I really want. He knows all about me, and he's still there, barely out of reach, allowing me to hurl myself at him all I want. And I'm not even paying him any more—not in cash, anyway. Sometimes I imagine myself as a groupie, following this repulsive rock star who lets me get just close enough to rip buttons off his clothes. He doesn't know my real name, but he'll certainly screw me one of these days. Which is just what I want—not for him to screw me, but for him to let me screw myself.

So that's what I really love most: hating me. The man who helps me do it is the only lover I understand.

"Pain," he scrawled on the bottom of her last page, "is one hell of a basis for a relationship. On the other hand, *fear* of pain is no basis at all. Face it: if she were here, could I even tell her she matters to me? No. Foxx."

He found the foil, wrapped what was left of the meat, and then stood uncertainly in the middle of her kitchen. Put it in her refrigerator? Freeze it? Take it home to *his* freezer? That was when he noticed the little jar with the violets. *Bitch*, he thought. Typical damn asinine transparent bitch, trying to pull that kind of a stunt. Then he remembered that she didn't know any stunts, which made him even angrier.

He stuffed the pot roast into a paper bag, and

then into his briefcase, along with the clean shirts and the paper on "Clinical Depression." Halfway out the door, he dropped the briefcase, wheeled back into the kitchen, emptied the water out of the little jar and took the violets too.

His place had acquired a faint smell of disuse. Except for seeing patients there, he had all but moved out weeks ago. Telling himself it was timesaving, after all. Matter of convenience. Not to mention how much easier it was keeping track of all the things he couldn't seem to find without her help any more: yesterday's mail, his sunglasses, the shopping bag with all his tax records for 1971, last night's paper that he meant to clip an editorial out of. She said it made her feel better, having all this stuff in her bureau. She would sit there counting the socks, like a greedy child checking the candy haul after Halloween.

A cleaning woman still came on Tuesdays to swipe at his overflowing desk with a dirty chamois cloth, and to run his aging Hoover across the footprints—but with steadily waning enthusiasm, it was clear. He felt a stab of conscience about the plants. Neglect had bleached all the scarlet out of the coleus and the Wandering Jews. The avocado seed had spontaneously aborted its latest shoot, rather than bring it up under these conditions. The others, wan faces lifted to the sun on the dusty sill, looked cowed and sullen, like a class forbidden to act up no matter how long the teacher's back is turned.

Once he had bought a scrawny rosebush in the country, for $1.49 at the A&P. He planted it halfheartedly, not expecting much, and then watched the damn thing burst into flaming life. Shooting off giant pinwheels of roses, one after another, like a time-release spansule. Once in a while he had fed the bush, or given it an acid bath, but mostly it sat there fending off its own plagues and pestilences, expecting nothing much from him. It seemed content with its bad bargain, as if it had decided, for its own quirky reasons, to throw in its thorny, beautiful lot with a strange psychiatrist whose nurturing instincts were erratic at best, and even then, clumsy. Why was it the plants in his life always managed to take him as is, and still thrive, while the women in his life, never?

He switched the telephone-answering machine to "Playback." One message was on it, from her: "Hi . . . just, I love you." He made what she called his clenched face, the one he reserved for her grossest acts of inappropriateness. Such as clutching at him in front of old friends who would later have to be set straight about his not being seriously involved. People who would have to be told firmly that despite their impression—no, really—she was just this . . . someone, he was . . . seeing.

Love, of course, was the last word in inappropriateness. Sooner or later it was also a word every woman used on him, or tried to. Flung it at him, usually, like a ransom note, without spelling out the "or else." As if her uttering it could force him to pretend the word applied. *Love?*

He always tried to explain why not. Why not even the *word*. Patiently, and in advance. In plenty of time to avoid. A thoughtful driver lowering the brights well before the other car gets close. He would long since have told them that the word was too variable, too imprecise. You let a word loose like that, someone could get hurt.

"What *I* mean by it is something very precise. And it's very precisely not something *I* feel." What *they* felt might be something different—probably was; in fact, he was almost positive they must mean something different from what he would mean if he said it. So he did not mince the word. "I don't love you, and I won't *say* I do just because you'd like to hear it, or because you said it first. It would be lying. It would be *inappropriate*. It would be unfair—to *you*. Don't you *see?*" They never did.

So sometimes he'd segue into Harry Stack Sullivan, just to prove that he, Foxx, wasn't the only precise one. Sullivan had a thing about love too. He said the word applied only when you valued another person's happiness as much as your own. Not *more* than your own, unless you were a saint, a nut, or some other extremist type. But definitely not *less* than your own. If it mattered less, then whatever it was, it wasn't love in Sullivan's book.

"What would Sullivan say," she had asked him once, "about a woman who kept giving her all to a man who seemed deliriously happy taking it, but incapable of giving anything back?"

"Sullivan," he replied gently, "would say the woman was either a saint or a nut or other extremist type, or else she would eventually stop wasting herself on a bastard like that. Why?"

"I just wondered," she had said, and rolled over to finish crying on her side of the bed.

The fact remained, however, that by Sullivan's standards none of them had ever loved him. Including her. Even she admitted wanting something back. Eventually she would want everything back, because that was how it worked. And he would not have it to give her, then any more than now.

"Well, but what *do* you feel?" she had asked, another time. "Nothing?"

"No, of course not nothing. Of course *something*."

"But what, then? What is the *appropriate* word you and Sullivan use for . . . *this?*"

Meaning, he assumed, Listen, you bastard, we have screwed, you and I. We have been screwing steadily, and you've wanted it, and I've given it, and what the hell have I asked for except that you use this *word*, which as I see it you damn well *owe* me? For starters.

"I . . . care for you," he had offered lamely. ". . . fond of you, concerned about you . . . you're number one—how's that?"

Rotten, was how it was, apparently. How could number one be anything but rotten, when the number she wanted was unlisted.

Chapter

FIVE

HE MEANT TO get a really early start this Friday. In fact, if he weren't on the road by two, he knew there was no point trying at all until midnight. It seemed to get worse every weekend now, so that he could tell by the tension of people's faces Thursday how bad it would be on the expressway Friday. The entire city seemed to arrive simultaneously at the peak of its tension/anxiety state. Nothing relieved it except being the first in the office to get onto Route 495.

It was a considerable source of pride to Foxx that he never had to start for anywhere at the same time anyone else did. Out in Laconic Beach on Sunday afternoons, he could sit in his back yard with his rosebush, watching the long caterpillar of homebound traffic crawl painfully past his house, until its lighted tail disappeared in the darkness, leaving the road clear for him. In the city he felt the same smug sense of control about seeing patients at seven in the morning. By the time every other man he knew had gulped his coffee and sprinted for his train, he had already earned $45 and was still wearing his bedroom slippers.

So this Friday, when he aimed the battered green VW bug confidently toward the Triboro Bridge and checked his watch against the lighted numerals over the Tip Top Bread factory—1:55—it was disconcerting as hell to discover a minute later that the key to the Laconic Beach house *wasn't* in his jacket, after all; he must have worn the brown sweater coming home last Sunday. Furthermore, he couldn't find the other half of the last Dexedrine tablet he had deliberately left in the bottle for the trip out; he must have screwed the cap on loosely, so that it had fallen out, and now it was two o'clock on the nose and the express toll lanes on the bridge were filling up, nobody moving, and he suddenly wished he could U-turn the hell off and go back to find—all right, damn it, her.

He flipped the radio on. The traffic eased a little suddenly; it had only been some poor bastard boiling over, blocking a lane. Maybe he had put the house key in that can of tennis balls he never took out of the trunk all week. Maybe he wasn't as tired as he thought. Maybe everything would be all right if it had to be.

He should have brought someone out for the weekend. Betty Jane, maybe. At least Betty Jane would have cooked something Armenian tonight, and not draped herself across him in public tomorrow like a flag on a military coffin. For a change he could have had a date who wouldn't become catatonic the instant there was a party, or even one other person in the room—as if by retreating into stony, moon-eyed silence, she could make him shut out the world too. A date who wouldn't keep whispering "Please, can't we go home? I need, I want . . ." until finally he had to desert her totally, and she'd end up drinking too much or passing out, or just sitting there reproaching him with her big sorrowful eyes, from the other end of the room, like a grieving stone madonna in some Byzantine Pietà.

After three weekends of scenes like those, Dr. Foxx's latest girl had earned herself a nickname in Laconic Beach. Chuckles, they called her. Chuckles! It was perfect.

On the other hand, Betty Jane had borrowed his car, got a ticket, and then refused to pay it. A matter of principle, she said. She had double-parked outside Woolworth's, where she'd gone to buy him a dozen wooden pants hangers. Okay, maybe he had asked her to pick up some hangers, but had he asked her to double-park, without leaving a note in the damn windshield? On Urgent Medical Call—Woolworth's. Either that, or she could have gone shopping on the damn subway, like everybody else.

All the same, Betty Jane would have been a good idea this weekend. She might even have finished

wallpapering the kitchen for him, a project she had
started two weekends before they broke up over the
parking ticket. He still had two double rolls of the
paper she'd picked, and one and a half bare walls
in the kitchen. Chuckles didn't care for the pattern.
Little roosters and frying pans. Ych, she said. Even
if Chuckles could hang wallpaper, she wasn't about
to pick up any torch Betty Jane dropped. Not in his
kitchen, anyway. Not with little roosters and frying
pans on it.

So be it, he thought, sighing. There really wasn't
much point patching things up with Betty Jane for a
lousy weekend and two rolls of unhung paper. Besides, he knew damn well he'd end up having to pay
for the parking ticket. After which—he could hear it
now—Betty Jane would say "I love you."

By Saturday he was feeling better. The weather
was great and so was his tennis; he hadn't played
this well all summer. At five o'clock, flushed and full-
sweated after two blistering sets of doubles and an
extra hour of singles, he was ready for anything Laconic Beach had to offer. Laconic Beach was no longer offering it to him, exactly, but even if he noticed,
he wasn't letting on.

The men who'd played tennis with him scurried
briskly off the courts, into their late-model cars and
home to their sand castles, firm-bellied wives or firm-
er-bellied weekend dates, and their frosty tall glasses
of icy whatever, with pieces of fresh floating fruit.
Within fifteen minutes, they knew, Connie Foxx
would be chugging up one of their driveways in his

disgraceful car, with half his laundry spilling over the
back seat, four racquets and fifteen cans of balls
wedged between the grocery bags that were full of
unsavory stuff he either had not yet unpacked this
weekend, or had not yet thrown out from last weekend (no one ever ventured close enough to find out
which). Usually there was a girl too, someone ter-
rific-looking who must be crazy, or why would she be
crammed in Foxx's junk heap among all his other
dubious treasures.

Foxx's summer friends kidded him unmercifully,
or clucked over him like estranged parents. Still, they
always took him and the girl in, with barely audible
sighs. What did he say her name was? Poor baby.
They took Connie Foxx in because no matter how
miserable they were, it made them feel better just
looking at him. This successful, handsome, charming
psychiatrist, of all things, who shivered on their
sandy welcome mats like a bedraggled lost pet, waiting to be let in out of the warm.

Whatever they were having was just what he
needed most. Another drink, a handful of carrot sticks
or macadamia nuts, a shower, an invitation to lunch
tomorrow. He would hang around till they stopped
refilling his glass and began pointedly discussing where
they were going for dinner. If they were going for
it right there, if the portable barbecue was already
warming up on the rear deck and the sirloin marinat-
ing right out on the butcher block, or the house guests
coming back any minute with the lobsters, they
would have to be very pointed indeed. Would he

take potluck? He would take the all-time potluckiest, if they let him.

He was so adept by now that he knew what awaited him at every stop, down to the size of the Cheez Bits and the number of ice cubes in his glass. The Marksons would have four house guests, all vying for Most Effusive against Charlene Markson, their hostess, who had held the title for fourteen years. Charlene would press Connie Foxx to her ample bosom like the prodigal he was. She would press fresh tidbits into his mouth and stale tidbits into his ears, until he was sated enough with the Marksons to last the summer—at which point, hungry or not, he would somehow force himself to leave gracefully, on the ground that he was . . . uh, expected, elsewhere on Beachplum Drive.

He would push relentlessly on to the Winklers, who would have sour-cream dip and matching faces, and the Murdocks, who would have enormous chilled pitchers of rum punch and twelve pale business associates of John Murdock's, because this was the weekend John had to conglomerate, or diversify, or dissolve, or possibly all of those.

Fortunately, there was a large party Saturday night. In Laconic Beach, large meant that the hosts were hiring one of the beach clubs, importing a caterer and inviting everyone within a twelve-mile radius, including the bad fairy, if any, just in case. And the theme would be Chinese or astrology or maybe Moroccan, with couscous flown in from a Queens restaurant called the Casbah, and old Charles Boyer jokes, and the women would toss veils over their bikinis, and the men would wrap beach towels around their heads, and they'd get a local live rock band called Ylleb Recnad, which everyone would know right off was belly dancer backwards.

Tonight's hosts were Bobby Shaftow and L.J. (Little Jack) Horner; L.J. had been dubbed "Little Jack" at the age of thirty-seven, the first season he had rented a summer house with Bobby Shaftow. Before that the L.J. had stood for Leon Joseph. Bobby and L.J. were Laconic Beach's answer to the late Aly Khan, or the early Baby Pignatari.

Each had two divorces under his belt, along with a mild ulcer and an incipient paunch. They renewed their bachelorhood vows together every summer by renting an even bigger house than last year's, with an even odder-shaped pool, and bringing out a fresh batch of girls who could be changed every week, along with the satin sheets, for a small extra charge. The girls were always pointedly busty and pert, their heads carefully weighted for balance with teased bouffancies and glistening extra lashes. Their thick frosty lipstick never caked because their little tongues were constantly darting out to lick something.

Foxx always enjoyed studying L.J.'s and Bobby's girls. Psychosexual dynamics of the breast stroke, as practiced in king-sized water beds. The use of lace-edged panties for flouncing across the back court during a men's singles game. Little thong sandals with plastic flowers between the coral toes. Different hairdos that slipped on over the professional frosting they paid fifteen dollars for on Friday, and then subjected to too much sun, sand and sporting with L.J.

and Bobby, so that even for twenty-five dollars it wouldn't have lasted till Saturday night.

Under the heavy lashes their eyes always appeared too wide to be anything but terror-stricken, until you realized that this was the way the girls drew them on. The ones who came back several weekends running seemed to bring more and more explicit outfits, into which they changed more and more frequently, as if they were raising their voices. In fact, the voices did rise too, acquiring a thin edginess just short of hysteria if they were still around by Labor Day. They rarely came back to Laconic the following year, unless a fresh L.J. or Bobby Shaftow had washed up over the winter.

The theme of tonight's party was Organic. The invitations, on recycled toilet paper, said "Come as Something Pure." Bobby's girl, the color of one-hundred-percent wild-clover honey, had poured herself into a handmade macramé sarong, and big hoop earrings formed out of natural dried-apple rings. L.J.'s date wore a delicate chain of soybeans around her bare waist and a film of clear cellophane from neck to ankles; she had modestly folded it double around the pubic area, though someone might have told her that two times nothing equaled nothing, even there. All night people would be pinching to see if she was really biodegradable.

Predictably, the menu was full of wheat germ, sprouted mung beans, fertile eggs, goat cheese, seven-grain bread and carob cake. The rock band was billed as Compost Heap, and the drink of the evening— rum, yogurt, fresh-squeezed carrot juice and a dash of ginseng root—was called Pure Shit. It was a smash.

"Where's Chuckles?" Bobby and L.J. asked him, first thing. They were both wearing natural-linen jumpsuits, open to the waist, and white handcrafted leather sandals with buckles that tinkled when they walked, like last laughs.

Foxx volunteered a noncommittal shrug, clapped them both on the back, mumbled "Great party," and went over to say hello to Lee Risley, the painter. Last fall Lee had stormed out of the Racquet Club, of which she was a founding member, in a typical Lee Risley tantrum over the club's rules pertaining to women. "1. No women allowed on court one, ever. 2. No women allowed anywhere during prime time (Friday afternoons, Saturday and Sunday mornings, all holidays)." "Fuck you too," Lee announced tersely, posting it on the bulletin board below the new rules, and promptly resigned. This spring she had installed two beautiful clay courts behind her pool, and so far had not invited a single Racquet Club member over to play. Except Dr. Foxx. "Hey, Foxxy," she'd call to say, "free brunch." He never refused. Lee Risley had the odd assurance of having been born rich, spoiled and sexy, and of having quickly acquired a permanent distaste for any man who was awed by a woman like that. Including her three husbands. Foxx was not in the least awed, which made him mildly diverting. He didn't blink when she talked, either; as a psychiatrist, he was no longer impressed by foul-mouthed women.

Every weekend Lee had at least two professional tennis bums as house guests and/or studs—well-

67

known ex-champions of one circuit or another, mostly named Buddy or Pancho or Tony or Nick. They would spend the weekends giving Lee a variety of runs for her money—on the court, in the pool, at the parties, in bed. Mostly she beat the little white pants off them everywhere but on the court; mostly they took it—and her—beautifully.

"Hi, Foxxy. You know Pancho? And Buddy? You wanna come play tomorrow? Unless Whatshercunt wouldn't like it. You could even *bring* Whatshercunt. She'd sit quiet and watch, right? I could give her crayons and paper. Free brunch, Foxxy?"

"She's not . . ." he started. "I haven't got a date this weekend."

"Aha."

"So I'm . . . available."

"So to speak," said Lee, winking at Pancho.

On an impulse Foxx took her hand and led her away to dance. Compost Heap was playing "Born Free." Lee was startled enough to lean against him, and he tightened his hold on her bare tan back. She was wearing something very thin and soft, and her body molded itself into his hands like a perfectly gripped racquet.

"Foxxy boy, you'd like to be full of surprises," she whispered. "Wouldn't you?"

He caressed the naked back in lieu of returning the ball. She reached behind her and drew both his hands away, but then pressed closer, still holding them, sliding them along her body, against her breasts. Then she lifted her head slightly and laughed.

"Lee?" he said.

"Yes, Foxxy, I know. You're available." She laughed again, softly. She might never take the set, but she was ready for every one of his strokes.

They left the party in separate cars, because she'd be damned if she'd set foot in his "Shitwagen," and she'd also be damned if she'd entrust her new Mercedes to Pancho and Buddy. Presumably they'd get back to her house somehow, and if not, not.

She had some champagne on ice in the pool house, and she wanted to rally for an hour and then take a swim. When she'd had enough tennis, she stripped off her shirt and shorts, finished the champagne in her glass, and without a word, dove naked into the pool. He sat for a while at the edge, watching her pale neon body flash past him underwater like some exotic sea anemone; then he dove in too. Their bodies floated together, drifted into each other, and then apart, like waves. She raked her nails down his back languidly; the pool lights played eerie shadow games, and neither of them spoke. The whole scene had a surreal gray-green luster, like the negative of an erotic underwater documentary.

Suddenly she laughed, ducked his head down toward her thighs and held him there, treading lightly. After a minute, lungs bursting, he tried to push her away, but she had her fingers laced in his hair, and she wasn't ready for him to come up. He had an instant nightmare of her holding him there like that, locked inside her, until he drowned. "Well, *shit,* your honor, who the hell would have thought a psychiatrist couldn't perform under water?"

That night he had the old dream about his grandmother and the puppy—the one he wanted for his eighth birthday. He had begged them all: Granny, his stepfather, his mother. "Oh, please," he begged. For something alive that would love him.

And when the day came, his grandmother drew him up on her lap and said, "Close your eyes, Sandor, *draga sagom*." My darling. And he felt the tiny paw scratching his back. "Oh, Granny!" he cried, spinning around, his heart bursting with love. But there stood his grandfather, holding a little red stick shaped like a hand. It was a Chinese back scratcher. They all laughed.

"Is it nice, Sandor?" his grandmother said. "Come, *draga sagom*, it's for you! Happy birthday."

He had climbed down slowly from his grandmother's lap, swallowing the pain like hard poison candy. It was not that they had denied him the puppy; it was the laughing! In his sleep now he could still feel that tiny paw scratching him. He could still hear their laughter. "Look, Sandor! Is it not *oyen szep?*" "Yes, Granny. Very beautiful. Thank you."

The next morning, drying himself in the shower, he noticed the little marks on his back. For a minute he forgot where they came from: Lee Risley had broken the skin with her nails.

Chapter

SIX

IN HIS MONDAY mail he found another long letter—twenty handwritten pages. They were in a stamped envelope, without a postmark. Hand-delivered? By her? Over the weekend, he'd run into a writer who knew her, and who had heard she was in California. Her phone had been temporarily disconnected. She had quit her magazine job a month ago; Foxx knew she had some free-lance writing assignments and "possibly a book," she had said. "Possibly a novel." She had refused alimony from Harry. "I'd never ask a man for money," she explained. "Once I heard my sister-in-law ask my brother for five dollars, and he said, 'What did you do with the five dollars I gave you Tuesday?' "

He knew she had a small savings account, and a habit of selling things to friends—her typewriter, her grandmother's turquoise beads—if worse came to worst, which it occasionally did. The fact was, she *liked* poorness. Adolescent striving for independence, was how he'd sized it up when she'd been in therapy. Her father was the principal of a small-town Michigan high school; her mother taught seventh-grade math. They would have helped, but she would have died before she let them. "I manage," she said indignantly, with the cute bravado of an eight-year-old runaway as drawn by Norman Rockwell. Solemnly packing eight dollars in nickels, three peanut-butter sandwiches and a map showing where the best roots and berries grow. As her therapist, he had decided to leave it alone; she was coping, after all. So far, she had coped with almost everything except growing up. And being happy. And learning not to screw around with her analyst.

TO DR. FOXX: UTTERLY CONFIDENTIAL
MY TURN
TOPIC: WORK—TRUE AND FALSE

One of the problems is that I never questioned it when I first heard the saying, "Woman's work is never done." If I accept it as a basic truth, then what am I doing sitting down? Shouldn't I be up swabbing something? Isn't that a film of grease on the countertop? What about the water spots in the sink? What do you mean stainless steel?

I once heard a joke about a nun to whom Jesus appeared in a dream and said he was coming to visit her humble convent. She ran to waken the Mother Superior. "What shall we do?" she asked, trembling with reverent excitement. "Look busy!" snapped the Mother Superior.

I spent my life trying to obey that holy order. I rarely talk on the telephone unless I am also rinsing dishes. Why is it, my own mother (Superior) asks me, that every time I call you long distance, regardless of the time of day, all I can ever hear is water running?

Why? Because, holy mother, I am washing away the sin of idle chatter.

My real work, writing, has never been fraught with any such guilt. Nobody ever checks on my real work. I know there are spiteful strangers all over the world whispering about the dust in my apartment, but no one gossips about the fact that I only wrote three pages today instead of fifteen. No one cares if I write no pages. When am I going to dust that apartment, though?

My favorite question that is asked only of women is "What do you do with yourself all day, now that the children are in school?" Or "now that you have a maid (to do your work)?" "I write. I paint. I meditate. I masturbate." "Really?" they say vaguely. "That's nice. At least it keeps you busy."

Where does it come from, this firm, guilty belief that I am flouting higher laws? That my real work is not writing? That I am not, in fact, doing any work at all unless I succeed in getting the rust stains out of my toilet bowl?

A few months ago I called my great-aunt, who is an artist, and mentioned that I had been busy working. She said, "Oh, you poor thing!" And I laughed and said no, that I was really quite pleased because I had just finished a major magazine piece. And she said "Oh!" again. "When you said 'working,'" she explained, "I thought you meant cleaning the house!" As I said, this great-aunt is an artist.

Of course, when I had an office job, nobody doubted that I was working, because I left the house. If I were a male writer who stayed home all the time, would my great-aunt think I was cleaning? Would anybody be checking my dust?

I lie in bed with my notebook, and sometimes I fall asleep. If someone rings the bell at 10 in the morning or 2 in the afternoon and wakes me, I am overcome with shame. I dash cold water on my eyes, fix my clothes and try to look busy, lest they think me a lazy housewife. They'd never think me a lazy writer. The real world is full of laziness: cops asleep in patrol cars, garbage men stealing cans to avoid dumping them, magazine editors drinking lunch, repairmen making noonday passes at housewives who would rather they fixed the TV set in time for Secret Storm. But only a woman writer in a messy house would ask herself how she can sit there writing when there's so much work to do.

Yesterday a meter reader rang the bell. I felt I had to explain myself. What was I doing at this hour, looking groggy and disheveled? It's not what you think! I wanted to shout. Let me explain! He gave me this knowing look; he actually grinned. "Sorry to bother you, honey," he said. "You go on back to sleep now." It was noon. "I wasn't asleep!" I cried. "I was thinking!"

I should tuck a pencil behind my ear before I answer the door. That way they will at least assume I'm someone's secretary. "That's all right, honey," the meter reader said after my outburst. "Wish I could go back to sleep, too."

I blush; he is right, of course, and I am a liar. I am a lazy housewife, just as he thinks I am, married or not, gainfully employed or otherwise. My sheets are not changed regularly; my laundry sits in the silent dryer, wrinkling; I run out of eggs. Yet I am forever sponging and wiping away the evidence. I spend a third of my life wielding a Handi-wipe, like a defense weapon.

I never saw my mother with a sponge in her hand. Our house was clean; people were hired for that. My mother taught school, and felt no shame. Her house, her record, her hands were clean. I own twenty-eight sponges in different colors, and four dozen bottles, jars and plastic containers full of wax and promises. I collect them like jewels, for I know they will bring a low luster to my surfaces and restore my original finish with a scent as fresh as lemon, mint or pine. They will exert panel magic. My worn spots will sparkle and glow; my impurities will dissolve like bad memories in a sink full of tears. I stand in the housewares section reading labels, seeking salvation for $1.09. Something there is that will foam away my dull, lifeless conscience and leave my brain unclogged, if used as directed.

It gets worse when I'm not actually stringing words together like a child with a play jewelry kit. When I'm not making something with my word kit, I am prostrate with guilt and cleansers. Am I atoning for not writing? Or for having tried to be a writer when I was put on this earth to clean?

"What is it she does now? Look how she rubs her hands."

"It is an accustom'd action with her, to seem thus washing her hands."

Yet here's a spot.

TOPIC: FACES

I am trying to give up cosmetics. All cosmetics. If Dr. Foxx loves me then, he will love my actual face, not the one I have been palming off since I was 16, like the personality that I elevate with Dexies before inflicting it on an unsuspecting public. My actual face is never seen by the naked eye except for my own and my cat's.

I thought it would be something like giving up chocolate, I mean, about as hard as that was but with the same positive feeling during the process. Look at me, I'm getting thin and pretty, I could say, pinching myself under the ribs every hour or so to verify it.

Chocolate was a symbol of my fat self, so I knew that once I beat chocolate, I had the whole thing licked. I never went back to chocolate after I gave it up, but I still think about it. I still taste it somewhere in my mouth. At the movies sometimes I can feel the ghost of an Almond Joy bursting open in there, flooding my inner cheeks with such inexpressible almond joy that tears come.

And I think about Beryl, in my dorm, who used to keep her whole desk filled with Hershey bars. I mean, she filed them, on edge, in different drawers, according to size, and with or without nuts. The center drawer had nothing in it but this one giant bar, a plain one, so that when she did her homework she could break off a little square every 20 minutes as a reward. Every 10 minutes if she was doing geology.

Beryl was practically six feet tall, so no matter how

many little squares she took of an evening, nobody would ever dare call her a fat girl. She said. At 170 pounds, she would draw herself up and march around the room, declaring, "There goes that big Beryl. Big, not fat." I believed her, but I was only 5 feet 7, so I never kept more than a single regulation-size bar in my desk, and I bit only during geology.

I never considered my chocolate problem out of control, not even when I got a D in geology, but it took me over a year to kick Almond Joys. And that was a snap compared to kicking make-up.

Make up. Meaning invent. Make up something more accptable, because that face you have on right there will not do, I'm afraid. First I tried giving it up just for quick trips to the supermarket. Stark naked. Eyes and mouth. Out on the street, in broad sun. No hat, no tinted aviator glasses. I felt people staring. Of course, they weren't really nudging each other. They weren't whispering, "Look at that person's eyes! They're not at all lush-lashed, did you notice?" And have you ever seen anything so colorless as those lips of hers? Ych."

One night I cut out a Marlboro Man from a magazine ad and tried to picture a Marlboro Woman instead. Now, I thought, what if her eyes were accented by those nice weathered crinkles, just like that, indicators of a hard, adventurous, outdoorsy life? Would Marlboro Woman run back to the ranch house to apply a little moisturizer? I knew damn well I would; just for the picture, I'd say.

Why, though? Who is it for, this forged masterpiece of a face I keep creating? For men? Not if I know them very well. If I'm married to them, say, or if we have slept together long enough for the mascara to wear off.

Women, then? Well, maybe my mother. "Why do you look so tired?" she'd ask, whenever I wasn't made up. And I'd cringe. "Why are you so pale? You need more lipstick." I need more lipstick?

Strangers in the street, I think I could handle—eventually. After all, they don't know who I'm supposed to be. Maybe it's okay with them if I'm not lush-lashed. They're not lush-lashed either, and I don't hold it against them. Maybe they appreciate that.

I make up for people I know—but don't trust. People I talk to at parties. Face to false face. People who (I believe) will either like me or not, depending on my skill with roll-on eyeliner. Of course it's crazy, but then why am I still afraid? Is Golda Meir afraid to face people without roll-on eyeliner? Why does Bess Myerson reshape her eyebrows into arch enemies of consumer protection? And just when did Golda Meir discover that she didn't need roll-on eyeliner?

See, that's the tricky part. I know I wasn't born believing I needed any of that stuff, not even lipstick. Even in the deepest slough of my teens I didn't wear a complete facial disguise. I accepted my face, whether I hated it or not. I thought of cosmetics as something special to put on, in both senses, like a party dress.

I wonder when it stopped being a game for me, when it became unthinkable to go out the door without the put-on.

I remember playing Desert Island, in which you told what you couldn't survive without if you were shipwrecked. What cosmetic. You would tell how you could wash your hair with rain water, and rub berry juice on your mouth, and polish your teeth with sand. Leaves, of course, could be twined into simple body coverings so you wouldn't get a nasty burn on the

*delicate parts. Low tide would be your mirror, and
sunshine would correct your tiny complexion flaws.
What I would rather have died than be shipwrecked
without was my tweezer. Without a tweezer I knew
my eyebrows would gradually knit together like a
great black line slashed across my ivory forehead,
and when the rescuers came I would have to go hide
in a cave.*

*But why is it I don't feel I have to make up a face
for a man I love, the person I should be most in fear
of losing? Why should he be the one who sees me
plain? Why don't I sleep propped in position, eye-
shadowed and rosy-tinted like an excellent embalming
job, so that he will always remember me that way
when he falls asleep?*

*On some level I guess I am fatalistic about it. Either
he will wake up and love me in spite of my face (just
as he loved me last night in spite of my body), or he
will leave because he doesn't really love me and
there's no point in staying up all night to prevent the
lip gloss from smearing for a man who's leaving anyway.*

*Look at what I accept from him in the way of im-
perfection. His brows can scraggle; his pores can clog;
he can be really filthy-looking when he needs a shave.
He can have unslightly hair almost anywhere, tufts
of it even sprouting from his shoulders. I don't like it,
but in no way do I consider that he needs to have it
removed.*

*Anyway, I now go to the supermarket, and for short
walks, wearing only my bare face. But not to a party,
not where I still think other people will stare at me,
and where I will cringe whether they do or not.*

*Oh, and I gave up going to the hairdresser. I wash
my own hair now, not in the rain but in the shower,*

and wrap it around my head until it dries. It looks all right. It grows and shines, and is actually nicer than I used to think, when I had it "done" every week. I don't even mind so much if it curls up and dies in humid weather. I have learned to forgive my hair. What will I do when it turns gray? Can I accept it gray? All of it? I could accept Dr. Foxx's hair all gray. I think it would be sensational. I already accept the first signs of creases across his forehead, furrows between his eyes, and deep worry lines beside his mouth. I think of it as a world-weary face, and terrifically sexy. What if it were my face, though? Would I lift it? How far up? God, I hope I won't ever think I "need" to do that. I figure if I can give up make-up now, then when I'm 50 I'll be ready for the face I deserve, the face that was waiting for me all along. My old face.

TOPIC: CUNNILINGUS

In California I met someone called Jonas, a screenwriter who always drives too fast with the top down, and keeps the music on very loud in his apartment, even when he goes away for a whole week, so that when he comes back it's still playing. He's afraid to turn anything off. At this party where we met, he came over and said, "You're cock-struck, aren't you?" It was because of the way I held the stem of my glass; he'd been watching me. I was holding the stem between two fingers and sort of running them up and down. He said a woman should always hold a cock like that, lightly, unless she was holding it with another part of her body. He was extremely sexy; he said all this stuff in a very quiet voice, and he had a wild, childish look, a strange haunted face. He re-

minded me of the boy who was supposedly raised
and suckled by wolves. This Jonas also had a very
long body, almost too long. Fragile, like a Giacometti
statue. And a damaged mouth. Bruised, I thought, or
else operated on during infancy for a cleft palate or
something. But it wasn't ugly; it was sort of beautiful
and fragile, like the rest of him.

Later he said he wanted to kiss me—there, you
know—and after we did everything else, we did that.
Not hungrily, but very passionately; I mean, he was
really doing it for himself. I couldn't bear it; I kept
wanting to scream "Why, why, are you doing that, it
must be terrible down there!" I kept wanting to pull
him up by his fragile hair and rescue him. Prince of
Darkness. I was numb; I couldn't feel anything.
Shame must be a local anesthetic. I was sure any second he'd emerge and say something devastating from
which I'd never recover. But when he finally did come
up, he said, "God, I love doing that to you," and I
began crying hysterically, I don't know why. Disbelief
—"What do you mean I've been accepted at Rad-
cliffe?" Like that. What did he mean he loved doing
that to me? He must have meant he hated it. That
would be your subtle irony. Or else he hated me;
that would be heavy irony. Didn't he see what I
looked like? Was he a pervert? Teen-aged boy rapes
82-year-old widow. Living Giacometti sculpture ap-
plies mouth to portion of woman unfit for human con-
sumption. Insane screenwriter samples waste products,
declares: I love doing that to you.

Now Dr. Foxx would never. And I'm not sure how
I feel about it any more. You can't really compare it
to how I feel about doing it to him, because I like it,
in a way, but I think only in a masochistic way. It's
one more superb sample of our many services, sir. We

are justifiably proud of our fellatio. Like our cooking, it is the result of painstaking attention to detail.

Oral sex may be only a civilized form of cannibalism; that's what some foreign scientist said in a treatise somewhere. He thought that was why America was so obsessed with it. Savages. I think it's probably just another sign that we never grow up. Oral is moral; if you're good I'll give you a lollipop; we are stuck with our sucking; penis as pacifier, nookie as nipple. Of course, Dr. Foxx is not oral at all (he's anal), so in his case that's probably that.

It's possible that I don't really taste any worse than he does. Still, I'd never ask. Maybe he's afraid of the dark, or of all those scarlet tongues leaping. Or the deafening silence, except for feathers rustling. Birds of prey. Maybe he thinks of it as trying to go home again. Last time he was there, his mother rejected him. Threw him clear, banished him with violent force. Maybe he remembers. Maybe they're all afraid we'll only toss them out again, howling. Maybe Jonas really was suckled by a wolf.

When he finished reading, Foxx sat holding the letter for a long time. He sat in his analyst's chair, facing himself. She was right, of course; he'd never offered to do that, not once. Frightened? Possibly. No excuse. Her husband Harry had told her flatly, "I don't like to"; and that was apparently that. The fact was that most men didn't like to. It rarely came up in analysis. He tried to think of the last time a patient even mentioned it. Most women didn't expect it, after all. No, that wasn't quite fair. Maybe, like her, they did, but would die before they said so.

What if they did say so? Wasn't *she* saying so, in a way? The only way she could?

"Forgive me" he scribbled across her last page. Not that it would change anything, even if she were there at that moment. "What's to forgive?" she would say, shrugging it off. And they would both keep the answer to themselves.

She had been home for days. Not exactly home, but in town. On the plane she had decided not to go back to her apartment. Foxx's socks would still be there in her bureau drawer, rolled up and piled like a child's arsenal of dark woolly snowballs. Or else they would be gone; he would have *confiscated* them. Either way, she didn't want to open the drawer.

So she would stay with Tess for a day or so, and then maybe Sophy and her husband would take her in until it was time to go back to California. *Penchants Magazine* had asked her to do a piece on Arnold Hatch, the author, whose new five-million-dollar contract for an unwritten novel, tentatively titled *You Mothers*, had just made him the richest two-finger typist in the world. Hatch was still fleshing out his own character into something a little more colorful; currently he was living with two of his three ex-wives, including the one who had shot him. What *Penchants'* editor wanted was an irreverent look at the Hatch ménage (they had run a *reverent* look last year), with a searching analysis of the ex-wives—how they felt about each other, about him, and about the two-hundred-odd other women, presumably imaginary, who inhabited Hatch's fictional world. *Penchants'* editor—along with almost everybody else—

knew perfectly well that those two hundred broads were in no way imaginary, but genuine flesh-and-hot-blood souvenirs of Hatch's real-life adventures. *How the hell does he do it?* was what *Penchants* thought its readers deserved to know. All the Dirty Little Secrets of Success. A Hatch job.

She could have made it up without leaving New York. Even if she went, it would *read* as if she'd made it up. But *Penchants* paid well, and the book she had started—her novel—had suddenly stopped dead on page 26, like Dr. Foxx's car after a heavy rain, and another week in California would at least be another week away from the telephone, which she found herself picking up three or four times a day, dialing the number and listening to his recorded voice on the answering machine. "This is Dr. Foxx. I am not in my office now, but you can reach me at—"

She would hang up at precisely that point, because otherwise she would hear him give a number to call, and she would call it and reach him, but not really.

Hello, he would say (guardedly). How are you?

I'm . . . I love you. (She wouldn't be able to control that.)

Silence.

Do you miss me? (She would say that too, she knew it.)

I know you're there. I know you're somewhere.

Do you want to see me?

Of course.

Ask me, then. Say, Please, I want to see you.

Look, I can't play this game right now (ever); I'm working. I'm at the hospital. I have a patient. Do you want to see me? Is that why you called?

I don't know. I'm . . . sorry. I didn't mean . . .

So it was much better not to try reaching him at the other number.

It was inevitable that Dr. Foxx would lose the ten crisp twenty-dollar bills he had hastily stuffed into his tennis shorts; he knew it even as he stuffed them. He had not wanted to leave that much cash lying around the house, because he always kept the doors unlocked out here. In the city he religiously locked everything, both house and car, even if he was only going out for the paper, or double-parking in front of his own building with the doorman on duty. But out here he made a point of *un*locking, to signify a kind of devil-may-carelessness appropriate to weekend living and exurban freedom from fear. He would try to persuade himself, or some other, possibly higher, power, that one could neatly exorcise all New York evils with the turn of a country key. Since he was never truly persuaded, however, he would then spend frantic minutes throughout the weekend seeking ingenious hiding places for valuables, just in case one evil had a summer place in Laconic Beach. He would go around laboriously tucking and sliding bills and checks into blanket chests and telephone books, under tennis socks in the hamper, or between magazines in the brass coal bucket—and then promptly forget where the hell. Or, worse, as in this case, concealing whatever must not be lost in some pocket or inside his racquet cover, and carrying it with him, so that, finally, there was no chance whatever of not losing it.

He did get his watch back, though. He had left it in the Racquet Club shower room last weekend, and somebody had turned it in.

The problem seemed to be growing worse. He admitted this to himself, but he wasn't up to confronting the underlying causes. Not this weekend, on top of losing two hundred dollars. Maybe another half a Dexie. No, maybe just clear the head with a Benzedrex inhaler.

Friday's mail had brought another thick envelope from her. On Saturday it was still on the floor of the car, unopened, under the front seat with the new *Medical Economics*, yesterday's *Times*, and the latest outrageous computer-error cut-off notice about his electricity from Consolidated Edison. By now these dispatches of hers were arriving every three or four days, washing up on his rocky shore like bottled SOS messages from a desperate shipwreck survivor or an orphan no one will adopt. Whoever finds this, I love you.

He decided to read this one at the club, in full sunlight, while waiting for a fourth for doubles.

TOPIC: WHEN I GROW UP

Of course it was a man—Vonnegut?—who wrote about the day you wake up and discover that your high school class is running the country. But I have that feeling too. The first boy I kissed is the head of a company that makes two out of every three lamp switches produced in the United States. My brother's best friend in the eighth grade, who swiped the key of my secret diary when I was 9 and loved him, is running for Congress. Even the girl who told me my first dirty joke (about a man searching for his car inside a lady—could that really have been it?), a joke for which my mother washed my mouth with soap—the girl who told it to me has her master's in anthropology and is raising four children in a trailer in New Mexico in order to do fully funded research on Indian tribal history. Whereas I am still trying to decide what would be good to major in that doesn't involve any 8:15 classes.

I have narrowed it down, of course. That is, I no longer expect to be a Rockette. I still would, if they asked me, but I know they aren't going to, and I am not even devastated about it. In fact, I realize it is a good thing I never really got as far as the fat man in the greasy hat who did all the hiring at the Radio City Music Hall, or at least was in charge of auditioning the girls. You know, to the point where that man told me, around his wet cigar, to lift up my skirt, girlie, way up now, that's it. And where he then shook his head—I know even now that he would have shaken it—and said thank you, girlie, meaning no, of course. It's a good thing that I didn't go on practicing four hours a day, which I started doing at the age of five, on my professional tap-dancer's board that was said to have once belonged to Eleanor Powell, a historic board made of narrow oak slats cleverly hinged so you could roll it up and store it in the closet when you were through practicing—only I never wanted it rolled up because I might want to practice another hour or so after supper. I had a solo number, "When

You Wish Upon a Star," in the recital at my tap-dancing school; I had wanted the "Lady in Red" number, but one of the older girls got that because she had a Figure. But "When You Wish Upon a Star" was okay, better than okay, there were only four solo numbers altogether, and I was barely 6 years old, not to mention tone-deaf. I was also in the military number; I was only in the chorus for that, but it was a very tricky routine, and so was the Scottish one, a really fast Highland Tap Fling, and that one had my favorite costume, a black and silver top with a very short pleated kilt that twirled like a skater's skirt, and a jaunty hat with plaid streamers, and we all looked so synchronized, with our black and silver arms flashing out across our bodices and the last angular dip forward, each with one silver shoe raised behind us for a count of 10.

Coming home on the bus the night of the recital, I had to keep everything on: the big spangled cardboard star on my head fastened with a satin band, and the white satin and tulle fairy-tale ballerina dress with a sweetheart neckline, and the silver shoes, the new ones with one-inch heels, and all the theatrical make-up and the little pin-spots of fierce light in my eyes, spangled stars to match the headdress. The people on the bus knew I was magic. I refused to sit down even though there were seats—not to crush the tulle, I said, but really to make sure they all saw me standing in the spotlight that I was sure was still following me. "When you wish upon a star, makes no difference who you are . . ." I believed every word of that song, I had sung it that way, with my whole heart and utterly tone-deaf, and with a tiny potbelly in my tulle tutu. The whole audience of grownups in the Knights of Pythias Temple, who actually paid admission for the recital, clapped for me when I made six successive whirling turns, perfectly balanced, clean taps one-and-two-and-brush-out-stamp, and I sobbed through the whole second chorus, "Everything your heart desires will come to you," because I was so good, they loved me so, that they had clapped right in the middle.

I never for a single minute wanted to be any other kind of star, just a Rockette. Only as soon as I told my parents that I was serious, that I really did not want to do one other single thing in life except practice two more hours every day on my board, so that I would be—they immediately took me out of Frankie Fallon's Tap-Dancing School, because it was high time I got interested in ... well, boys, for instance; I was pushing 12, I ought to be dating like my cousin Cynthia and how would I ever meet any boys if I spent every minute of my life running through the military number one more time, just the last turn and dip, and with the costume on, so you could see, brush-out-two-three.

It took me maybe a year to stop crying every night in bed, but after a while I thought, well, maybe a swimming star—not a racer, but in a water ballet company. A floating Rockette, sort of: Eleanor Holm instead of Eleanor Powell. But I was already too fat, and pretty soon I realized that I would have to walk past the audience before diving into the pool, and take my bows standing out of the water in a bathing suit. I couldn't just materialize like a mermaid in the water, doing my underwater gliding routines and executing my perfect scissors kick that carried me clear across the pool. But then, what could I do? What else could I do for which people would clap so hard it would make me cry?

Painting. Really startling work, very dark, with strange long-haired women hanging themselves in prison cells. Perhaps painting. Full moons over eerie landscapes with the ghosts of gravestone crosses. She has an undeniable talent—sinister, brooding, but undeniable. Undeniably a demonic genius.

However, my art teacher in high school pointed out that I could not draw a nose. Even at the age of 15 I could not do a face where the nose was anything more than two little black dots. What was wrong with that, I screamed; look at Picasso's noses, I happen not to like the nose, two dots is all I wish to portray, I am entitled to my own vision of the nose. Picasso, said my art teacher, knows how to draw a proper nose. Once you have mastered draftsmanship, anatomy and proportion, you may reject it all and go back to two dots; nobody will say you do it that way because you cannot draw a nose. I gave up painting shortly after that.

Actually, I never really felt the same about water ballet or painting as I did about tap-dancing.

TOPIC: GUILT

When I imagine this panel of judges in flowing robes, curtsying to each other before assuming their places on the bench, I can think of only one kind of guilt I don't have: straight sexual guilt. I think I must have been born too late for it. I don't think I ever felt guilty for having a sex urge, for indulging it, or for tasting myself. (That must be why I don't have the classic rape fantasy—I don't have to quiet my puritan conscience.)

But except for sexual guilt, I would say I have a complete set—the basic seven-volume edition. One for every day, like the pastel panties that used to come rolled up in a celluloid box.

What I feel most guilty about is shopping. Really bad is buying something that costs too much (according to what standard, knows God, but I know when it is too much), and so I take my evil purchase home and let it stay in the box for a while, aging. That way I can make believe that I didn't really buy it yet, it is not used, it can be returned for full credit, so what I have done is really not so bad, not yet, anyway. See, I haven't even taken the tag off, the bill from the store won't come for weeks, it doesn't count, I still have my fingers crossed. Once I wore a periwinkle-blue triple-ply cashmere cardigan that cost $40. I took it out of its box and wore it without removing the tags; I tucked them neatly inside the cuff and the back of the neck. I could feel the cardboard, could hear it warning me whenever I turned my head, but I moved very carefully, stood ramrod straight and held my arms well away from my body, did not lean back or perspire in it, or bend my elbows against the creases, so that when I got home I could lay it back in its tissue paper, in its box, in its shopping bag, with its sales check, and go on pretending I had never bought any such thing as a $40 sweater.

Dirtiness is the other big one. I know exactly how much dirtier I am than most people. Of course, I was really filthy in college, but so was everyone else then. I never washed anything. I had a closet (it was the first time in my life I'd ever had a closet in which no adult would ever set foot and ask what all that filthy stuff was doing in there) and I would pile things up in there and when the pile reached the height of the closet pole, I would take everything out and rearrange it, on the theory that the older dirty stuff on the bottom was now fit to wear again, having aired out for some weeks. There was one year when I hardly ever got undressed. I wore the same clothes and slept on top of the bed, which therefore never needed making, and felt really disgusting, which was very satisfying.

Dr. Foxx has this hang-up about the sheets and pillowcase; he does not approve of lying in bed, or even on top, with your outer clothing on. I have to pretend I'm not actually touching the pillowcase with my sleeve; I am suspended above it; I levitate.

When I was a child I was made to take a hot bath every night, followed by my dose of cod-liver oil. I don't know whether it was the dread of the cod-liver oil that turned me against the bath, or whether they were equally awful, but I am mystified even now by stories in house-and-garden magazines about the sensuousness of bathing, of the bath as the sybaritic center of the home, if not the world. Even when the tub is pink marble and there are sixteen gold shower heads spraying perfumed oil in adjustable needle-massage sprays, and hothouse orchids blooming in the steam, I hate it. Wet, cold, shivering and waiting for the spoonful of cod-liver oil, is what I feel. Quick showers in the summer aren't bad, because they cool you. But they have nothing to do with liking to feel clean. Clean still has to do with good girl/bad girl, with clothes that need laundering, with changing the bed and guarding against smells, with feeling guilty because someone (male) may be offended, with knowing no one (male) will ever love me the way I really am underneath: dirty.

Finally, there is the guilt about obligations. I do not fulfill them—any of them, the simplest of them. Either I don't care enough, I'm callous, or I haven't got the simple ability to sense someone's need for me to do whatever it is that everyone else is doing with no trouble at all. I am incapable of responding if someone is sick, even a little sick; if there is a death in someone's family; if there is a new baby or a wedding; or even if they have only sent me an invitation requesting an R.S.V.P. I cannot form a syllable of the very first thoughtful word. My tongue is permanently tied, stuck to the roof of my mouth with peanut butter or paralysis. I stand mute in the presence of a friend's vulnerability, a hostess' graciousness, the most elemental social demand. Thank you, how nice, how sweet, how terribly thoughtful. Good luck, I was so sorry to hear, I was shocked and saddened by the sudden news, I had such a lovely time.

It isn't that I feel nothing; I feel something intensely, but I can't possibly tell what because I don't know the words. That is, I know the words, but they are not the real ones, and I have none of my own, not one. Why is it that every idiot in the world has a complete social vocabulary? Isn't that wonderful, I would be delighted. I want people to like me, but I know they won't, so I act and speak—or fail to act or speak—in the most unlikely, most unlikable, unspeakable way. And then, of course, they don't like me; in fact, they detest me. Even the most casual acquaintance learns in a minute what a terrible person I must be, and it proves—aha—exactly what I thought all along (I told you so): I am indeed detestable.

When I was married to Harry, I tried to give nice parties. Dinner parties, eight or ten, buffet style and cooked all by myself—beautiful, delicious food. Every time, I spent a solid week in advance nervous hysteria, consulting fifteen different cookbooks and shopping for a hundred dollars' worth of heavy brown bags containing ingredients for possibly a dozen combinations of elegant dishes, because I would change my mind again and again before the party. This dessert would be too gooey following that main dish, and what about heating the hors d'oeuvre at 350 degrees when the cake needed 400, and how on earth can you end up with three different concoctions on the same plate, all of which are white and gooey?

In the end I would spend all night in the kitchen, covered with grease like the stove, walls, and pots. There would be a mountain of crusted casseroles and other burnt offerings, and chaos on every surface, including where the dessert plates had been neatly stacked until someone helped me clear the dirty dishes and piled them on top of the clean. I could faintly hear the guests; they were always talking in the other room and I would fervently thank God that they were at least talking so that they could not notice how long I was gone, or come out to make sure that everything was all wrong. My cheeks were flaming; I would drink far too much wine and laugh high terrified laughter from the minute they came. I could barely even manage to say hello, never mind how glad I was to see them, because I was never glad to see them, not any of them. Yet I desperately wanted to be able to say whatever you were supposed to say, sure, throaty little phrases, with dry hands and sparkling eyes. Instead I stared at the rings on the table, because there weren't enough coasters, and the flowing ashtrays, which I should have emptied before dinner—but how could I when the cake was burning and the chicken running blood from the joint after three hours of basting and loving attention? No one would ever eat what I brought out, they knew I would poison them, and the cake knife would be tarnished, and the wine spreading on the white cloth. I wanted only to die.

Guilty of gross inadequacy in the simplest homely task. But what did I expect? I was the last child ever picked on any team for a relay race or a game of ball. I would have killed myself for the team, but it wouldn't help me catch the ball if it came—the only ball they needed me to catch, and I always saw it coming, flying toward me like doom, and their faces turned to me, hard, expectant, she absolutely has to catch this one, goddamn her, and I would reach for it and never, never . . . and no one would ever speak to me again.

I never once redeemed myself for the next time. I stood cowering with shame and certain knowledge of their contempt; however much I cared, I could not ever perform the rock-bottom minimum feat demanded of me. I could never call my parents just to say hello. I could never answer a letter. I could never do the kind of work needed to get an A. Yes, I know, Dr. Foxx said; notice me, pay attention, I am doing badly, I do bad things, take a firm (loving) hand with me, to me.

And with Dr. Foxx too. Is that what I want? You need, he said, to be dominated and loved by a man you respect.

I do? I said. Yes, of course I do, I nodded. I must need exactly that. We must all need that, we must want it too; in any case, we must all achieve it. And then when we have it, we must find out why it is so hateful, and why we still feel so guilty for resenting it and for still being angry because it is not, after all, what we had in mind.

What did we have in mind? Maybe we'll outgrow this too. It's probably just another phase. Why is this woman not smiling? Give her something to make her smile. Open her mouth and close her eyes and I'll give her something to make her shape up. Then she'll feel less guilty, and she'll finish the dishes and smile and say how nice it was to see you again soon, I hope you're feeling much, much *better.*

"Poor darling," he scrawled at the bottom of the page. "I see that old Foxx was wrong again: you do not need dominating. However, the love he recommended may still be a valid concept, worth pursuing. Unfortunately, he has had no personal experience with this. Foxx"

Chapter

SEVEN

LIKE MOST OF the men who belonged to the Laconic Beach Racquet Club, John Murdock played tennis as he did life—or, more likely, the reverse. Murdock's game was a replica of his remarkable career on Wall Street: flamboyant, occasionally brilliant, more often ruthless but imprecise. An A student who never did homework, and who admitted it with disarming candor, rather than pride. His brilliance, if that's what it was, could have been a matter of hiring the grinds and knowing enough to pay them well so that *they* would do the homework. The imprecision only mattered when they failed him, or when something closer to true brilliance happened to be necessary.

In tennis, Murdock had a rare losing style, which seemed almost out of place with the rest of his persona on the court. When his game began to fall apart, he became wry and philosophical, as if someone had prepared him for this, tipping him off as to exactly when the recklessness would cease to pay, so that he might as well steer gently into the skid, let it all go quietly, because it didn't matter a damn—because in fact it only amused him to be playing any game at all, since he really couldn't afford this kind of time.

Usually, around the middle of the second set, he would begin the descent: double-faulting on his serves, slashing his brutal forehand shots into the net or hurtling wildly out. Unlike other men who swore at themselves or threw their racquets, Murdock would crack small apologetic jokes—funny self-mockeries about born losers and impotence, the kind of jokes only a practicing millionaire would dare crack while playing badly on court one.

Off the court, it was said that Murdock enjoyed life to the hilt. But it was the hilt itself he enjoyed, especially the jeweled parts. The blade—the sharp edge of success—was only an introduction. He dabbled in lots of things besides the market: real estate, tropical fish, marriage, psychotherapy, textbook publishing, gourmet food. Lately he had been talking about developing tennis-club properties in the Caribbean. A chain of clubs dropped like perfectly placed lobs, each in the brilliant sandy center of some lush new island that would be perfect for next winter's vacation.

Dr. Foxx liked the sound of it. In fact, the more

Murdock talked about it, the more Dr. Foxx thought
he might be really in love with the idea. Dr. Foxx
had never exactly envied Murdock, though it must
have been partly that. The rest of what he felt was a
kind of fatal attraction, if not of moth to flame, at
least of industrious ant to dancing grasshopper. Murdock had certainly made his own way, but only after
what is euphemistically called a solid head start. Like
the cartoon character entering the leather-bound
sanctum of the men's club, inspiring two elder states-
men, enshrined behind their *Wall Street Journals,* to
lean over and trade respectful gossip: "That's young
Fitzhugh—inherited fourteen million and built it up
to a goddamn fortune."

On some level, though, Foxx sensed that his fasci-
nation with John Murdock had less to do with Murdock's success, or any mysterious magnetic aura, than
with his own childhood memories of rich, confident
boys like John Murdock—and of himself, the skinny
outsider in their midst, whose grandmother called him
Sandor, *draga sagom,* Sandor *eletem,* and lied about
his home address so that he could go to a nice school
with the rich boys downtown.

Foxx had grown up surrounded by Murdocks,
studying them from a wary distance and making sure
that they never knew much about him. Nobody ever
went home with him after school; nobody knew he
didn't live with his parents because his stepfather
didn't want him; nobody knew how ashamed he was
of the sound of his own name. He learned to hold his
own on a ball field or a tennis court. Later he dropped
the Sandor, became S. Conrad Foxx, M.D., and had

seven years of analysis, but it was still important to play John Murdock's game—and to beat him at it.

The funny thing was that whenever he watched Murdock on the court with somebody else, Foxx could predict every one of his moves. Yet when he was out there himself, Murdock invariably outfoxed him.

Today, for instance, Murdock had been ahead 4-2 and as usual seemed to have the set firmly in hand. Foxx served and Murdock swung hard, but somehow the ball dribbled off his racquet. Murdock stared at his racquet and shook his head. Foxx knew that psychologically this was the turning point. Now if he could just loosen up, could concentrate on blunting Murdock's terrific serve, stroke a crisp forehand cross-court, or send him a deep top-spin lob, he knew he could turn it all the way around.

What he didn't expect was that Murdock would start cheating. The first time Foxx wasn't sure. "Out!" Murdock yelled, miscalling Foxx's return. His voice had a thin fierce edge to it. Foxx stared at him curiously, but let it pass. Then Murdock kept forgetting the score. "Is that deuce?" he would ask absently, when it was clearly 15–40, and Foxx would have to recall the points for him.

Then Foxx was serving again. Murdock started to swing, then stopped and called it out. This time Foxx said, "I'm pretty sure that was in, John."

"Well, take two, then," Murdock replied quickly.

"No," said Foxx. "Either the serve was in, or it was out."

Murdock stood silent for a split second, apparently calculating something. Finally he turned and shouted at the spectators, "Hey, anyone see that?"

"Well," said Vic Tanner reluctantly, "I thought it was in."

Marty Cooper nodded.

"Okay, then," said Murdock, smiling. "Your point, Doc."

Foxx promptly double-faulted his next serve, and lost the game. Even after he'd taken the set, 7–5, he felt acutely uncomfortable. On the way home he realized why; he had not wanted it to be true about Murdock—not quite so true, anyway. He had been fantasying all week about the Caribbean tennis-club operation and about maybe going in on it with Murdock. Plotting week-long trips in bleak February weather, checking out the newest investment with his own racquet. St. Maarten, Eleuthera—places he had never been able to think of a good excuse to visit until now. He could work out a couple of tours of West Indian mental hospitals, a talk or two to local psychiatric groups, and there it was: a fully deductible yearly winter vacation.

Of course, he had heard the stories about John Murdock; everyone had. Last week he had asked Marty Cooper what he knew about Murdock's business dealings, and Cooper had replied succinctly, "He's the only shark on the Street who keeps piranhas in his dining room so he can study their eating habits."

A few men Foxx knew slightly claimed to have been personally hurt by Murdock. Nothing cataclysmic, just staggering losses in what had seemed like a healthy market. Most of the alleged victims didn't want to talk about it in detail; they only said vaguely that Murdock simply hadn't quite leveled with them while their ships were sinking. "*Down?*" Murdock was supposed to have said, whenever they called him nervously at his office. "*What* down? Oh, that! Well, of course I knew about *that* weeks ago; of course, it's absolutely nothing, I promise you, just a little settling down is all that is, I happen to know there'll be a complete turnaround by the, uh, fifteenth."

And then on the twenty-second, when they cornered him out here, lounging around the club pool, say, he'd tell them to relax, for Crissake, it was nothing, hadn't he *told* them it was nothing? "First thing you've got to learn," he would say loudly, "is how to float on your back." Diving in and exhaling a stream of confident bubbles, he would say, "Like me." Then he would duck underwater to swim across the pool in incredibly long strokes, surface at the other end and shout, "By next week, at the outside, you'll see. Complete turnaround, I promise you."

Or he'd invite them home and pour fifteen-dollar-a-bottle wine into their fragile goblets, frowning sullenly above his mirrored aviator shades because the wine seemed a little warm now, out in the sun. With a great flourish of disgust, he would empty the contents of two whole bottles into the pool, and send his wife inside for two more, properly chilled, for Crissake.

Invariably the victim, whoever it was, would relax then, trying to float on his back like Murdock—until he went under. Part of Murdock's charm was the way he could blow those bubbles until everyone else sank, and then turn around to wave from the other end of the pool. He never seemed surprised to find nobody waving back. They sank to their doom not because they were all fools, but because nobody ever wanted to believe how much of a fool John Murdock could take them for.

Yes, Dr. Foxx had heard those stories. Nevertheless, when Murdock called later that day to invite him to dinner, he deliberately put them out of his mind and thought some more about what he had personally observed this morning. He knew all about Murdock's game, he told himself. Anyway, he knew enough; he'd been warming up for it all his life.

This summer the Murdocks had rented the Folger house. It was rumored they paid the Folgers $20,000 for a short season. The Folgers were supposed to have gone to Europe, but at the last minute they'd decided to summer in Laconic too—renting an old farmhouse with another family for something like $2,500, and pocketing the difference. Right after Labor Day they'd move back into their own house and throw themselves an enormous welcome-home party. Meanwhile Alex Folger was at the Racquet Club every weekend, and John Murdock graciously played with him, even inviting him over for a rum punch and a swim in his own pool. The chances were that Alex would plow his profits back into the market, so if Murdock played it right, he'd end up with the $20-000 back anyway, reasoning wisely that it pays to be nice when you pay that kind of rent to that kind of landlord.

Three limousines had brought the Murdock
ménage out from the city on Memorial Day. Wife,
three children, luggage and help. A separate car with
van had followed with the aquaria—the tanks and
filtering and heating equipment. Murdock had both
salt- and fresh-water collections, and it was true about
the piranha. He kept all ferocious specimens isolated
from the other species; he even had special tanks
fitted with interior glass partitions for the Siamese
fighting fish, so they could see each other but have
no physical contact. A well-known marine zoologist
had been invited out for the weekend just to help
him set up the tanks, which took up the whole glass
wall at one end of the Folgers' huge living room. Since
the tanks were all glass, with mitered corners and no
metal joints, the effect was spectacular; you could see
the Folgers' entire garden through them, so that the
fish appeared to be swimming through trees and
flowers, as though in a submerged tropical rain forest.

Murdock's current wife, Diane, was said to be an
extraordinarily difficult woman. In Laconic Beach,
"difficult" might mean anything from lack of interest
in tennis to embarrassing public displays of ill tem-
per. Diane Murdock was apparently given to both;
entire summers would pass without her ever appear-
ing at the Racquet Club, even as a spectator, and
one night last year when John unexpectedly brought
home eight fellow players for dinner, Diane had announced coolly that the refrigerator and bar were
both empty. Then, equally coolly, she had hopped into John's new Porsche and taken off. If John was per-
turbed, no one could tell. He had immediately called

thirty-two more guests and then telephoned some posh restaurant in the city to bring out an extravagant midnight supper for forty. Nobody remembered seeing Diane come home, and by Sunday night rumor had it she had spent the weekend at Van Cleef & Arpels, raising the bill for John's impromptu dinner party to something in five figures. As Murdock himself had said after his last divorce, for some men it was economically sounder to lease a wife by the year.

Tonight the evening was altogether delightful. There were ten people for dinner, and Diane had apparently expected them all, because there was plenty to eat, all of it excellent, and the wine, properly chilled in Baccarat crystal buckets, flowed as smoothly as John Murdock's conversation. Unlike any other stockbroker Foxx had ever met, Murdock talked knowledgeably about almost anything but stocks. In fact, the only time he mentioned the market all night was when he pointed out his latest Coral Sea specimens in one of the tanks. "That one is a Moorish idol," he said proudly. "Goes into shock easily. I can always tell when the Dow-Jones has dropped twelve points just by looking at him."

Foxx finally tossed him a few direct questions about in-and-outing, just to see if Murdock knew anything at all—or maybe just to show that *he* did. Murdock gave him straight, simple answers and a remarkably level gaze. "Whatever I don't know," he said, "and God knows there's plenty I don't, I can always find the man to ask. That's my secret—always has been."

In spite of himself, Foxx was tremendously excited when he left. Murdock had told him—reluctantly—a few concrete details about the new venture, Tennis/Carib. The first club was scheduled to open in November, on Barbados. Of course, he would check Murdock out further, he thought, first thing Monday. Then he smiled, remembering what Murdock said about doctorfish. See those knifelike spines on each side of their tails? he had said. Doctorfish always put up a beautiful defense. Murdock had a two-inch-long scar on his right hand to prove it.

Dr. Foxx did not sleep much that night. He kept seeing "Occupation: Tennis Conglomerateur" on his income-tax form, and balls bouncing on pink sand, and John Murdock smiling through a coral cloud, yelling "Out! Out!" Murdock was clutching something in each hand—some kind of fish. Foxx squinted, trying to recall the species. Then he remembered; sucker catfish, they were. Look at that mouth he's got, modified into a sucking organ? Murdock had said. Hangs right on to the aquarium glass, scavenging. Finally Foxx heard his own voice calling to the spectators: "Anyone see that? Anyone at all?" And *she* was there, in the front row, also smiling. "*I* saw it!" he heard her cry. "Oh, I *saw* it! Me, please, me!" So they both asked her, "Well? In or out?" And she smiled again. "In," she said, "on one condition: I'm coming with you to Barbados!"

In the dream he shook his head. No. He would beat Murdock all by himself, without her; that would show her who needed who. She had walked out on

him, hadn't she? Like everybody else. Well, so be it.
He would show them all.

On Sunday morning he called Murdock and
asked if there was still time to get in on Tennis/
Carib. Tentatively, of course; he'd have to check some
things first, of course, and see if he could swing the
cash. Murdock had said $75,000. John wasn't sure if
it was too late, but he would certainly try. And jug-
gle a few things around himself, if it wasn't too late.
Whatever, he'd get back to him on Monday, sure
thing.

Sunday was when Dr. Foxx lost the ten twenties
out of his tennis shorts. He refused to consider it any
kind of an omen.

By noon Tuesday, Foxx was a limited partner
in Tennis/Carib, with full membership and lifetime
playing privileges at T/C Barbados, the flagship club.
He and Murdock had exchanged a flurry of papers
and notarized signatures (Murdock dispatched all his
urgent correspondence by limousined courier).
When the last signature had been duly delivered into
Murdock's hands, along with Foxx's bank check for
$75,000, Murdock called his wine supplier and or-
dered a case of Mouton-Cadet to be sent to S. Conrad Foxx, M.D., along with a sterling-silver corkscrew
engraved with the T/C crossed-racquets emblem.
Murdock had thoughtfully ordered an extra dozen of
them last week from Tiffany.

Chapter

EIGHT

"WHAT CAN I possibly tell you about my sex life," asked Arnold Hatch, "before we've fucked?"

"Nothing, I guess." She flipped her notebook shut and stood up, extending a friendly hand.

He laughed. She hadn't asked him anything about his sex life.

She pulled the hand back and turned to go. "Hey," he said, "look, why don't we grab a hamburger before we get serious?"

"Fine." Apparently she had won something. The editor of *Penchants* would think so, anyway.

Hatch was on one of his five phones, the green one. "Michael, this is Hatch." He pronounced Michael as if it rhymed with *Sieg heil.* "Bringing a young lady from New York. *Very* lovely, yes." He half rose and peered over his desk at her legs, just to double-check. Then he winked at her. "Half-hour, and we'll need two very seductive hamburgers, usual way. I *know*, Michael, forgive, but she just arrived, I mean she's still got her *seat* belt fastened. Appreciate it, Michael, thanks much."

He hung up, sighing. "Michael," he explained, "grinds the beef to order, *with* the seasoning. Pulverized green peppercorns, God knows what all. He usually demands a day's notice."

"For hamburgers?" She was definitely back in California. As Hatch grinned at her, she suppressed a mad impulse to say she hated green peppercorns, and just wanted it blood-rare, with ketchup. He was fingering his famous head of curly Roman-emperor's hair, murmuring to himself. ". . . fuck later," she thought he said. She decided not to have heard, and not to say "Pardon me." He exploded into another laugh; her silence must have amused him.

Hatch rang several buzzers on his desk, and three men in navy-blue suits appeared at the door of his office. Hatch himself was wearing an olive suede safari jacket, open to show his curly Roman-emperor's chest hair, and a thin gold chain with an animal-tooth pendant. Female animal, probably. "Let's give little Miss, uh, the ten-dollar tour," he announced. "Right? These"—he gestured vaguely at the men— "are my associates." Class was dismissed; he had swiveled around to the window and was brooding over Sunset Boulevard. On the way out she noticed there was no typewriter in his office and no pencil on the desk. She tried to picture him writing. Maybe he talked his books into one of the phones. The red one.

Two of the associates took her arms, and the third walked a pace behind. She felt like a material witness. The Hatchery—that was really what it said, in gold capitals on the solid walnut double door—contained a vast suite of offices, like an agency or a studio. Hardly a literary aerie, but then Hatch was hardly literary. Thanks to movie deals and TV serials based on his best-known works, he had graduated into media enterprise. The Hatchery contained, for instance, three rooms marked "Pool": one for typists, one for billiards and one for swimming. There was another enormous room coyly marked *Thimk Tamk*, in which Hatch's resident story and publicity consultants lolled on fur-covered water couches, presumably in the interests of clearer Thimking. There were also two screening rooms, one for X-rated adaptations, the other for hard-core originals; an editing room; a Royalty Suite (for the accountants to check the royalties); and a Reference Library whose walls were papered with Hatch's book jackets, printed on vinyl panels in thirty-four languages. *Foreplay* in Turkish, *Getting Some* in Japanese, and of course, his first and best, *A Rotten Way*, whose title was a quote from Hemingway's impotent hero Jake Barnes (". . . a rotten way to be wounded").

"Solid-gold Hatch covers, every one," quipped one of the associates. She smiled appreciatively. Besides the thesauruses, dictionaries, almanacs, encyclopedias and collected Hatch works, she spotted several well-thumbled copies of *Plotto: The Master Book of All Plots.*

"Could I look at one of those?" she asked. The associates exchanged lifted eyebrows and shrugs. She picked up the book and flipped quickly through "Opposing the Plans of a Crafty Schemer" and "Seeking Retaliation for a Grievous Wrong." Under "Becoming Involved with Conditions in Which Misfortune Is Indicated," she found: "A, seeking revenge against B-3 for a wrong committed by her husband, A-3, who is dead, finds that B-3 treasures A-3's memory unaware of his evil character. A could destroy the beautiful love and devotion of B-3 for her dead husband, A-3, by telling her the sort of man A-3 was. A, in a spiritual victory, decides to spare an innocent woman . . ."

"Hey!" she exclaimed suddenly. "Isn't that the theme of—"

One of the associates nodded. "*First Come, First Served,*" he recited. "One-point-five million copies, hardcover, not counting book clubs."

She riffled further. "Falling into Misfortune Through Mistaken Judgment: A has a delusion in which a certain odor, manifesting itself during a tragic experience . . ."

"That one—" the associate began.

"No, don't tell me," she said, but the associate was not to be stopped.

"*Deep Breath.* Eight hundred thousand hardcover—"

"Arnold Hatches a Plot," she murmured. "A, a novelist who runs out of ideas, places his faith in X, a mysterious little code book. Suddenly, in real life,

A meets personally a fictitious character, B, from one of his early stories . . ."

"Say, that's not *bad*," exclaimed an associate.

"Let's see," she mused. "He could call it . . . *Fuck Later*."

Michael's was one of those iniquitous dens full of authentic tartan-plaid upholstery, stag-horn antlers and the pungent smell of real black leather. A place where a man was said not to feel quite at home until he had undergone his first partial hair transplant, his tenth complete tax audit, and his twenty-fifth lunch date with someone young enough to be exactly what she was. Michael's was where, whatever they were telling, it was in mournful numbers. Three hundred thou. A million two. As Hatch remarked loudly when they arrived, the place was crawling with men who owed him an aggregate total of twice as much as any of them would live to pay his estate. In fact, he figured, if the bomb fell before the coffee came, he would be out about fourteen million, give or take. He *literally* figured it, with a leaky ballpoint on the snowy cloth, shooting murderous glances around the room and carefully noting the names of every single bastard he was into for more than a hundred grand as of last Friday. ("Barney Schrank over there—produced the *Outcast* series, right? Based on my character P.J. McCord, in *One More Big One*, right? Half a mil . . .")

When he was through checking his addition, Hatch leaned back against the tartan wall, exhaling satisfaction. "And that," he sighed, "is why I can't afford to worry about money. Why I got twenty guys on the payroll now who are *trained* worriers. You saw how *they* look, right? Terrible. All twenty of them worried sick. Could cost me another fortune for medical attention."

"Could blow the whole fourteen million right *there*," she murmured.

He looked at her sharply before laughing. "Cute," he said. "Really."

Halfway through lunch she decided, perversely, that she liked him. He was a cartoon, with his twenty-five-dollar shaggy haircut and suede duds and image. He made up a whole childhood for her; she could tell that it must be the hundred-and-first all-new version. The mark of a born storyteller. Born, he said, on a freight train somewhere between Monroe and Spencer, Va.—or at least abandoned there, by a mother who must have been riding the rails, looking for some long-lost hobo lover. Anyway, he was raised, he said, by the train engineer who found him in the cattle car. Until the engineer died in a wreck and left Hatch, aged eleven, on his own—aboard another freight, this time bound for New York. At sixteen he had earned and lost his first fortune, bootlegging grapefruit during a Florida rail strike. And so on.

Having once collected country and western music, she recognized a few elements from "The Wreck of Old '97" and other minor classics, but she let it pass. She felt remarkably sanguine about everything —the Lancers wine, the itchy plaid seat, the table-cloth full of bad debts, even the lousy well-done hamburger which Michael and his merry band of green

114

peppercorns foisted off on the Hatches of this world
for a cool $6.50, prix fixe.

A dozen of Hatch's closest acquaintances passed
their table during the meal, tossing "Howaya-
Hatch?" over their shoulders, through their clenched
pipes or plastic little-cigar holders. "Hey-Hatch-
howaya?"

"Did it ever strike you," she asked him suddenly,
"that 'Howaya' is a rhetorical question in here? I
mean, suppose you *had* an answer? They couldn't
possibly hear it from wherever they disappeared to
before they even finished asking."

"Yeah, well," he said. "The answer is understood.
It's 'Okay, how you?' and it's pronounced silent, like
the *f* in—"

"What if, though," she cut in neatly. "What if
the answer was 'Riddled with cancer. Cedars of Leb-
anon opened me up, took one look and closed me
right back up again.'"

He shrugged. "Who the hell wants to hear about
your aberration on the way out of Michael's after a
six-fifty hamburger? Hey, let's go home," he said
abruptly. "I'll show you some of my wives."

She couldn't remember the name of the one who
had shot him, but if it was one of these two, she
would bet on Barbara—the cool one, a businesswom-
an in the great square-back Rosalind Russell tradition.
Crisp slacks with knife-edge pleats, and matching
repartee. A charcoal brain, as Arnold put it; an-
thracite with narrow chalk stripes. He respected the
hell out of her. In fact, he had just hired her as a

full-time consultant to Hatch Enterprises, a move which his accountants found more horrifying than his entire outlay for entertainment in 1970 (the year he flew two planeloads of guests to Las Vegas for the wedding of his third ex-wife, Joanne; after all, he explained, Joanne was now the first and only wife he'd ever had *off* the payroll). Barbara's salary, on top of her alimony settlement, made her what one columnist called the highest-priced Hatchick in Hollywood.

Cindy, the other one, was the soft type, liable to melt in a warm hand. Even her clothes clung and whispered. She did a lot of walking around the gardens, Hatch said. She liked to watch the fountains light up in different colors, and she really appreciated the sculpture. The sculpture consisted of enormous privet hedges in abstract shapes, created, Hatch said, not by a landscaper but by a famous *real* sculptor whose giant welded-metal constructions were in the permanent collections of every major museum on both coasts. It was the first time the man had ever worked in privet. Hatch had to put him on the payroll, too—just to guarantee that he'd come back once a month and prune the damn things.

Inside the house, each Mrs. Hatch had left her mark on some corner, the way First Ladies tackle the Lincoln Room or the Oval Office. Barbara had created the hard-edged living room in steel, glass and black fur, plus a knowledgeable collection of important modern art. Cindy had concentrated on the master bedroom, every piece a period Louis, fat and bandy-legged and dripping ormolu like a bravely decorated general.

It was also Cindy who liked to talk about the women in Hatch's books. She had never been jealous for a second, she confided, all shiny-eyed. She loved Arnold's heroines, every one, "Because they're all *me!*"—except, of course, for a few of the early ones. Those were all either Joanne or Barbara, though. And the sexiest "other" women in Hatch's books always died—either by their own hands, or the hero's. Arnold had always been very thoughtful that way.

Hatch took them all to a party that night, a small, quiet affair which he apparently found inordinately depressing. When the music started, he brooded in a corner, watching Cindy float by in the arms of other ex-husbands. When it stopped he brooded in another corner, listening to Barbara pick daintily at other ex-husbands' brains.

"Hey, *Penchants,*" he growled at her suddenly. "Why don't we go somewhere and discuss my sex life?"

She grinned at him. "I thought that's what this was."

He had thoughtfully provided three limousines —one for them, and one each for Cindy and Barbara. "They don't really get along," he sighed with the resigned despair of a parent who has done his best.

They stopped first at a Chinese restaurant, because he *always* stopped first at a Chinese restaurant. "Spareribs," he explained, as if that explained it. They'd finished dinner less than two hours ago. He'd had seconds of the filet mignon, half of Cindy's chocolate soufflé on top of his own, two cups of espresso,

iced crème de menthe and four thin mints—and then
had asked for a Dr. Pepper. She decided that spareribs must be his version of Alka-Seltzer.

By the time they got to her hotel, he had
emerged a little from his funk and was funning truer
to form—lowering his great head and pawing the
ground or, rather, her brown silk evening pajamas.
In terms of Hatch's "fuck-later" schedule, it was now
officially "later."

"Pick up your messages, baby," he commanded,
gliding smoothly away from her at the curb and darting into the lobby. He mingled with the crowd at the
elevator, eyes raised with a bland expression to the
carved bronze indicator needle pointing resolutely
up.

Takes years of practice, that particular gaze, she
thought, glancing uneasily at the desk clerk who
handed her the room key. Not a trace of a smirk.
She wondered if he was on Hatch's payroll, like
everybody else.

In the elevator she tried thinking about how Dr.
Foxx would look at it. I'm on this assignment, she told
him in her fantasy. Working press. Marguerite Hig-
gins unhesitatingly pulling the ripcord as she jumps
out of the plane. Geronimo. I was asked to do a
Hatch job for *Penchants,* and that's what I'm doing,
right?

Foxx shook his imaginary head. She could see the
little all-knowing flicker in his eyes, which would be
gray-green in this light. Are you having fun? he asked
quietly.

I don't know, she replied, not meeting his gaze. I'm not *bored*, I'll say that.

Well, then. He shrugged. Have fun.

But—

But Foxx was gone. Her hour was unfortunately up, the elevator had stopped, and Arnold Hatch had an arm around her waist, one hand resting lightly on her pelvic bone, the other on her room key.

"Want some?" he asked, offering his pipe. Hashish. She shook her head. "Then come here, baby, and let's do you." He sank back on her turned-down bed, and she went to him to be stroked. "Baby," he kept saying, this millionaire writer of love words. "Baby." There was something she had meant to ask him before . . . What he wanted most, that was it. Mr. Hatch, what does a man like you want . . . most. She asked it now. He sat up, held her away from him and looked at her hard. She forced herself to look back, equally hard and steady. No flinching, even with her clothes messed, where he had pulled them. She wouldn't *touch* her clothes.

He blinked first. "Most," he said, "I want to have been here. And also *here*." He drew a hand lightly across her breasts and down her body, to the V for either Victory, or Peace, depending.

"Kilroy," she said softly, "was here," and leaned over him and began to take off the rest of her clothes.

She would be in charge of herself this once, she vowed. Just this once. She would—

But Arnold Hatch had not figured it that way. He had only penciled her in for a quickie—on his terms. So he pulled her down and pinned himself to her, collector impaling specimen. "Yeah," he gasped. "Yeah." And it was over.

"I have to go," he whispered hoarsely. "Baby." In case she needed that.

She forced a smile, but turned it away from him quickly, knowing it looked vulnerable. "All those wives," she murmured, "at the door with the rolling pin?" Lightly. Ever so lightly.

He got up without smiling back, and went into the bathroom. She got up too then, impulsively. Just not to be there, lying *down* when he came out. She stood uncertainly at the door of the closet; there was a hinged three-way mirror on the door, like in a department-store fitting room. She opened the wings and stood there for a minute, contemplating the three nudes, images of herself as a profane Byzantine triptych. She didn't hear him come out of the bathroom, didn't see him come up behind her. Suddenly, fiercely, he was there, spinning her around, pinning her now against the cold glass. "Bitch," he murmured into her hair. "Cunt."

She went limp, like a peaceful demonstrator under arrest. Still he dragged her down; he would not be cheated. She had been wrong; he had penciled her in not for a quickie, but for a rape. "*Cunt!*"

"Cock!" she wanted to scream back. Wanted to hurl that single scarlet monosyllable. Like cunt, short for contempt. What if I could only come by reducing him, denying all of him but that . . . prick. She said it aloud, finally, gasping with rage. "You prick." He laughed, and then he turned her over. "No," she said, "please. Don't."

He smiled to himself. He could spare her that, he supposed. Hatch could be generous. For a lousy thirty-five-hundred-word piece in *Penchants*, she would remember him generous. Fuck it. Fuck her.

He got up abruptly and began to dress; she didn't move. "Hey, *Penchants?*" he said, kneeling beside her. "You mad at old Hatch? Got carried away, was all. Baby?"

"PLOTTO," she said, almost inaudibly, into the brown-flecked tweed carpet, chosen for its ability to resist soil in heavily trafficked hotel rooms. "A, a writer, poses as a fictitious character who despises women, including B, who, for all he knew, might have been a person in real life."

He patted her hair and said maybe she ought to get up off that floor and put something on, or something. Anyway, he would call her tomorrow from the office. As he left, she thought she heard him muttering to himself just outside the door. "Crazy bitch" is what she thought he said. It reminded her that she had forgotten to ask which wife had shot him. It must have been Cindy, after all.

Chapter

NINE

SHE *would* CALL during his double session with the Tuckermans. Barbara Tuckerman, aged sixteen, had finally loosed a torrent of overt rage at her mother for silently enduring twelve years of her father's adultery. Dr. Foxx was genuinely annoyed when the phone rang, and doubly annoyed when he heard her voice, breathless and slightly scared. "Hi," she said.

"I'm in session," he snapped, regretting it almost at once. She really did sound scared, and he suddenly realized that except for the strange letters, he had not heard from her in weeks. "I know, I'm sorry, I just"—he could tell that she was fighting tears— "wanted to ask if you . . . I'm going to Vancouver.

To the World's Fair. I could take you, I mean for free. I'm going now to pick up my press pass. I can get free plane fare too, through . . . I mean, if you wanted to go"—she wound down, so that the end was almost inaudible—"with me."

"Fine," he said crisply, aware now that all three Tuckermans were staring at him, the tears still coursing down their faces. "Fine," he said again. "When is that?"

"I'm leaving Friday," she said. "For a week."

"Oh. Well, I can't tell you right now, I'm sorry. Call me at four-thirty." He hung up, frowning. Vancouver?

She slumped in the phone booth, dripping perspiration. She had no idea if she could get him a free plane ticket. Never mind; she would buy it and not tell him. A man likes to be swept off his feet. She opened the door of the booth to squint at the clock over the lunch counter: three-thirty. Might as well stay in the five-and-ten until it was time to call him again. An hour of looking at orange rayon underwear made in Hong Kong, and children's fake leather moccasins with pictures of American Indians on them made in Taiwan. They kept all the good things under glass now, no touching, even the thirty-nine-cent frosted lipsticks and the evil-looking metal eyelash curlers with forties-looking models on the cardboard, indicating that the same eyelash curlers had been lying in that very case since the forties, or else the company president was married to the model, now aged seventy-four, widowed, and still curling her lashes.

Fake rag rugs and air-wick sachets fitted with little hangers for your closet. *Everything* for your closet: rolls of fake cedar and Rubbermaid stackers for extra shelf space. Everything durable, pliable, disposable, and obviously essential. She liked hardware best. Blister packs, tubes of liquid steel—all kinds of liquid promising to harden into other kinds of liquid. Liquid aluminum, liquid porcelain, liquid plastic. Chrome by the tape that would melt right into your dented rusty car bumper Like New. Who would ever guess that was a dented rusty bumper under there? Aerosols. She had never thought "cellar door" was the most beautiful word in the English language; Aerosol was.

Epoxy. Ah, epoxy both your houses. And Molly Bolts and Polypropylene—definitely a pair of go-go dancers with silicone breasts.

At four thirty-two she went back to the booth.

"Hi," he said softly. "I'm sorry if I was abrupt before. Difficult session . . . this family . . ."

Already she was crying. Why did he have to apologize, didn't he know he must never apologize, never acknowledge hurting her? It was his tenderness she couldn't bear; the hurt was bargained for. But *he* wasn't supposed to feel—

"Oh, darling," he said gently.

She cried harder. "Don't."

He stopped. "What was all that about Vancouver?"

"World's Fair," she sobbed. "Futuro."

"You want me to go with you?"

She ignored the form of the question. I asked if

you'd like to go. Obviously I *want* you to; that's why I asked. You're supposed to indicate yes, you'd like to, or no, you wouldn't. It's not a matter of what I want any more, for God's sake. All she said was "Yes." Damn him. "Yes, I want you very much . . . to go . . . with me."

"All right," he said. "I'll have to cancel a lot of appointments. Unless . . . Well, we don't have to stay a whole week, do we?"

"No. We don't have to."

"Well, I'll see what I can do. Where will you be?"

"I'll call you," she said. She would not be anywhere waiting. She would not. "I'll call you . . . tomorrow."

"Darling?" he said.

"I love you," she said, and hung up quickly.

That night she told the group about Arnold Hatch, and they all jumped on her.

Sophy had just designed a poster for the Women's Mental Health Self-Help Center: red, with an arresting black-and-blue graphic that said "Sado-Masochism Is Not Healthy for Women and Other Loving Things." She brought it to show.

"Derivative," Laurie commented. "But nice."

"Women are not things," Wanda snapped. "Loving or otherwise. I really think you should change that."

"Women *are* things," she protested. "Until proved otherwise." Then she told them about Hatch.

"Self-abuse," observed Margot dryly, "is probably

no worse than heroin if you restrict your intake to the prescribed maintenance dosage."

"Was it boring, though? The sex, I mean?" Sophy demanded.

"How could it not be boring?" said Laurie. "Have you ever read a sex scene written by Arnold Hatch?"

"Well, but it *wasn't* boring," she said defensively. "At first—I mean before the . . . the rape part, I felt sort of free. I *liked* what I was doing with him. I even liked *him.* At least I felt free . . . of Dr. Foxx."

"Free, shit!" sputtered Margot. "Free is getting *out!* Out of jail, into something *else.* All you did was move your masochistic ass to a cell on another coast. S-M is S-M is S-M, right? Arnold *Hatch,* for Chrissake!"

"But—" she said, and then stopped. Because they were right.

They would have to drive to Montreal, and then fly to Vancouver. Only one Canadian airline would spring for two round-trip tickets, considering the really dubious press credentials. She had a bona-fide assignment from *Penchants* ("Heigh-Ho, Sex at the Fair"), and had palmed him off to the Futuro p.r. people as a contributing editor to *Medical Aspects of Human Sexuality.* Every doctor in the country, she had sworn to them, planned his summer vacation by *Medical Aspects of Human Sexuality.* So they got two coach seats from Montreal to Vancouver, and it was he who wanted to drive from New York to Montreal.

How they went didn't matter to her at all. In her head, the key was that he had said yes. Not to the trip; that was only what *he* thought. She knew better. Yes was to loving her, because traveling thousands of miles with her was a kind of loving. He needed an unreal time and place to begin; maybe they both did. People invented fairs and carnivals to suspend their disbelief in each other.

So Futuro would deliver them. A fair, set on the day after tomorrow, in a foreign city which might turn out to be Samarkand. Still, it was worth a try. At least they would spend their instant sci-fi eternity upon a moving platform gliding through wonders that would never cease because they were the kind of wonders that would never exist in the first place. Which was the whole point of them, and which was perfectly all right with her—better than perfectly all right, to be exact.

In the car, his ratty car, speeding at night on ugly highways, she watched her own windowed face moving swiftly across the western New York landscape, blackened hills and night rain imprinted on it like a sorrowful map. Flashing lights and the names of unfamiliar towns passing like desolate years, like crumpled messages or lists of small forgettable things to be sure not to forget today.

It was already unreal, that he should be driving her so far—transporting her across state lines. She smiled at that. For immortal purposes. And then watched the smile fade quickly into the merging traffic. Tomorrow in Canada she would be a different person; tomorrow in Canada they would set each other free. Afloat in magic buildings shaped like soap bubbles blown from the Pacific by a giant child. Buildings whose transparent outer walls were fragile skins reflecting rainbows, and whose inner fittings belonged to a surreal dentist's office—clean machines, white-capped smiles and swirling newly minted liquids for swishing out the last taste of earthly present that might remain in the mouth from yesterday.

Every night they would eat exotic splendid food in white-and-gold pavilions bristling with remarkable handwoven artifacts and sauces from everywhere in the unreal outside world. Fountains and lights and instant bougainvillaea blooming scarlet outside, and music piped from other ionospheres. Germelshausen and Brigadoon and Erewhon would be here tomorrow and gone the day after, along with fluttering pennants announcing the grand opening of still more unimaginable worlds.

They would stay in a small hotel with a wishing well and she would only wish to be brightly irresistible as any white pavilion or fountain cleverly lit from within. She had brought enough Dexamyls to outdance all the bubbly rainbows, and he must love her then, mustn't he? Futuro belongs to those who outdance the past.

Of course it was not quite like that at all. Not quite. Vancouver was its own white pavilion, the fair was very fair, and they were still exactly themselves, a long way from home. Every night in the small hotel she would fail to get any wish at all, and he would not understand why this should spoil the day. She would take all the small delights they had seen and done, tear away the golden foil wrappers and find no sweetness—none at all—inside. They had evaporated, like circus candy touched by tongues. And she would sigh or sulk or cry, and he would say for Chrissake, let's go home, then. What's the point? he would say. Why wasn't it enough? Never that he did *so* love her, only that being here together in this not-quite-miraculous place should be enough. Why can't we just? he would ask, and *because* was no explanation.

Then he would kiss her and hold her, and she would promise to be whatever she was not. Satisfied, was it? And every night they would make some kind of love, while he waited for the Meprobamate he had taken to let him go, since she would not. Holding her gently, damning her hold on him. While she lay beside him, the last string of her Dexamyl beads inside the day's last time capsule, bursting open one by silent one, all through the night, like galaxies of small false stars, all cold and much too far away for dancing on.

He dreamed. Oh yes, dreams. Of his mother singing did he want the moon to play with? And camp, where she sent him at five; she must have gone shopping for his moon, he had thought, and when she came to camp later with the man she had married, he ran, crying "Daddy," and the man held him stiffly away and shook his hand, saying "Men don't kiss." He was eleven before they let him have his puppy, and then they gave it away the next summer while he was at camp, even though he won all the cups there were to win. He played so hard, knowing that to win was to be noticed, and that was almost as good as being loved. But his stepfather still said he didn't want him with them, so he went on living with Granny, who said he was her whole life, and his mother came to visit and sang about the moon he could have if he wanted.

Maybe she had loved him in her way, but it had taken seven years of analysis to forgive her, and God knows he didn't expect anyone ever to make up for that moon, or whatever it was she hadn't given him, after all. Least of all did he expect it from this woman who now said she loved him, and who, he knew only too well—having analyzed her, for God's sake, only too well—was as damaged as he was. Damaged people cannot give each other love in Harry Stack Sullivan's sense of the word, let alone moons; they only *need* love from each other, and that was, as any psychiatrist could tell you, not the same thing at all.

In the mornings he would wake to find more of her letters; she must have written them during the night. Pages and pages of all the things she could not say to him except like this. When they could be light together, as sometimes they could, he would tease her about it. If we were together forever and ever, would you speak to me then? She would lower her eyes and shake her head. She would forever and ever write to him, and neither of them would mention the unspeakable things she said.

TOPIC: COMMUNICATING

Just before he fell asleep after we made love last night, I said, "I love your cock," and he said, "How come you never could say that before?" His eyes flew open when I said it, and he studied me for maybe a split second. Then he laughed, but not meanly, at how confused I was, and he rumpled my hair and pulled my face down and kissed me. I was so startled by his response, I couldn't say another word. I guessed he figured I had found my sexual tongue in California. Courtesy of Arnold Hatch, the four-letter wordsmith. In part, of course, he was right: California was the trigger mechanism, but who could have known how loaded the pistol was? I guess it will always startle me when he turns analyst. Not that I don't believe he is omnipotent, all seeing, all knowing. (I know better, but knowing has very little to do with believing.) Yet now I never expect him to analyze me so openly, and with such devastating clarity. It never occurs to me that he should even care enough to do that. I meant to say some other things last night, for the first time, but suddenly I was mute again. Then, of course, he fell asleep; start to finish, the whole scene could not have taken more than six minutes—that's all it ever takes.

What takes longer, infinitely longer, is the turning it all around. Making the hurt into something I can use for my own dark purposes. Studying the back of him curled in sleep beside me. Thinking, ah, what beautiful contempt in a back turned that way. Stroking it with my fingertips, very lightly, so I won't wake him, because then he would be angry, and I don't need anger for this fantasy; indifference is enough. Listening to him breathe—he is content, he cannot possibly care that I ache. Gazing at the back of his neck, why is it I think it so beautiful, necks in general being very dull things. What is it about the back of his neck that is so exciting? That it looks phallic? So does everything look phallic. But in his case—ah, his case, yes. There's nothing about him that is like anything else I respond to. Even his indifference is a fraud, of course; I know that. If he were truly indifferent, would he be here at all? Would he care that I did not sleep last night? Or whether I will be all right tomorrow, or what it was that he said last to upset me again? He does care. *Tomorrow he will call me darling and want me to be happy with him. After all, he has traveled across a continent with me for no good reason at all. Sometimes it does make him happy to see me happy, even though being the agent of my happiness fills him with terror.*

It is such a convoluted thing altogether, this relationship. Perhaps every relationship is. Do I want him to go on hurting me, or do I only expect him to? In the fantasies he continues to be contemptuous while using me. In life I want him loving and tender, passionately moved. Yet never once have I fantasied him acting that way—anyone acting that way. God, I'm tired of my fantasies. Why doesn't he know what I want him to do, if he is such an analyst? Why doesn't he know that I want him to touch me, with or without contempt, the way he touches me in the fantasty? He will never; tongue and fingers slowly, gently; never. And whatever I do, he will never caress me while I do it. Soft touching is all, just there, yes, and there. And tell me why he loves to, or what he loves me to do.

Why will he never watch me moving over him like a guardian angel, never reach for any part of me then, with his hands or mouth? Why does he close his eyes instead? Why can he never bear to watch me? What would it make him feel? Is he afraid he could never go back to whatever he was reading to avoid watching me? Back to sleep? Back to leaving me? What if all he could think of, watching me, was wanting me never to stop? What does he think would happen then? Would I hurt him, does he think? And how and where would it hurt? What harm am I capable of doing him? I wonder if either of us could ever tell.

"Then *talk* to me!" he wrote at the bottom. "Darers go first! Chicken! Foxx"

TOPIC: CHANGE OF LIFE

It isn't that I think patterns are irreversible. Mine, for instance, is completely reversible, which only means that I can turn it over, or backward, or inside out, to show the cross-weave underneath. You get a very nice variation of the design, but it was made with the same yarns on the same loom, after all, so how different is it, really? I'm afraid I am already becoming what I was always afraid I'd be, only older.

I have this premonition of my voice giving me away again, like a bride. The older I grow, the higher and faster I must talk, as though someone is pulling it tighter and tighter, like a face lift, to silence the gathering silence. Some people learn to talk less and in lower tones, as the pattern of their lives grows more and more unmentionable. If you're lucky enough to be ashamed to admit what is happening, you can lapse into a permanent thoughtful pause. It is good to be able to shut yourself up, or down, or out, at will that way. That's how I see myself reacting—or at least how I hope I will.

I wonder if I am not already beyond self-improvement. In the women's magazines they constantly advise you that what you need is to do something about

it. Men's magazines never tell them that; I suppose
men never feel they have to. Come as you are. A man
always will.

Why is it that a woman is old at least fifteen years
before a man?

TOPIC: ALONE VS. LONELY

The loneliest I have ever felt was the first night I
stood on the corner outside Dr. Foxx's apartment
house, shivering in the empty wind. Don't get up, I'd
said to him. Sleep; I'll find a cab. I kissed the back of
his head. Don't worry, I said, I'll just get right into
a cab. Mmmf, he said. I'll be okay, I assured him
once more; don't worry. He wasn't worrying. Mmmf.
He was asleep. His head did not turn, did not so
much as move when I kissed it. I closed his door softly and went out to find a cab at 4 A.M., and there
weren't any, and it was biting cold. Why are you crying? I snapped at myself on the corner. You told him
to sleep, didn't you? You insisted that he sleep. He has
a patient coming in three hours.

In the taxi that finally came, I went on scolding myself. Still crying? Stop it this instant! I hugged myself
to keep the ache in the center of my body; otherwise
I knew it would spread along each of my limbs like
a mysterious wasting disease. But, I sobbed, why
didn't he know I didn't mean it? Why didn't he pay
no attention to what I said? Stupid! I shouted. Whom
do you think you are kidding! You know he knew you
didn't mean it! You know he went on sleeping because
he didn't care whether or not you died tonight.

That's lonely.

Loneliness is also a matter of nights when you're
wide awake and wanting, but not necessarily wanting

to work, not even necessarily to talk or touch someone. Just to have this person within reach, in case you change your mind in the next few minutes. Like having the museums and theaters and three-star Armenian restaurants within ten minutes of your house, even if you never go to any of them. (Dr. Foxx never goes. He cuts out the write-ups of the plays and restaurants and files them in a manila folder, to compare with the verdicts of his own mind or taste buds, if he should ever decide to go. Eventually he may feel that the manila folder is tantamount to having gone.)

It doesn't work that way with a person. Having him there within arm's reach, or voice's, whether or not you're taking advantage of it; having him there as against having him somewhere else, or not at all, has more to do with lonely than alone.

When I was a child, alone meant hated. Hateful. I hugged myself then too—constantly, in my closet, whispering, "There, there, I still like you," which wasn't quite true either. Other children used to do a funny mime act involving hugging yourself. You pretended you were locked in a passionate embrace; only your back was visible to the audience, and you wrapped your hands around yourself and moved them slowly, sexily, up and down your back. You rumpled the back of your hair, and tickled your neck; you stroked and fondled; you made imitation love. There were always whoops of laughter when someone did it well. I always cringed.

Lonely was standing out in the middle of the gleaming gym floor while the captains of the two relay teams chose up, making horrible faces at each other because the one sneering knew that the other one was going to get stuck with you, and the one fuming knew that getting stuck with you meant his team would lose.

One of them had to get stuck with you; they couldn't leave you standing there bleeding tears; the gym teacher wouldn't let them.

When I was a child, lonely and alone were synonyms. They both meant you were the one who got stuck with yourself. You were the entire losing team. It never occurred to me that anyone would ever choose to be alone. What if I got to be captain? Would I choose myself? I still wonder if I ever will.

TOPIC: THE WORST THING

The worst thing anyone ever said to me was said by Harry's best friend, Marv. This Marv was known to be a very big swordsman, as they say. He was large and bearlike and presumably overpoweringly virile. He had a complete set of Mark Twain's and Hemingway's works, which he used to alternate rereading every midnight with his milk and saltines, even if he had a girl waiting naked in the other room. One night I asked him if I could borrow The Sun Also Rises, *and he said, "I never lend books to any gash."*

"Wrong!" he wrote. " 'The worst thing' is not the voice of a man saying he hates all women. The worst thing is the silence of a man who can't say he loves one. So there. Foxx"

They had been in Vancouver four days before they could get into the Russian pavilion for lunch. The hit restaurant of the fair was in an extraordinary building designed like one of those colorful Ukrainian wooden peasant dolls with a babushka, inside which there is another Ukrainian peasant doll, which contains yet another, and so on. And there at the next table was Hal Eiseley, the wire-service reporter who had been her best friend on the first newspaper job she'd had, in Newark, right after she graduated from college and was still thirty-two pounds overweight. Hal had gone on to *Newsweek*, and she had gone on to Dr. Foxx. But he recognized her right away and came over and kissed her hello, and joined them for lunch, and she was really glad to see him, because, among other things, he was one of the few people she had ever known who was positive she was going to grow up to be a terrific writer some day.

They were having sour-cream blinis when suddenly, for no apparent reason whatsoever, she burst into tears and couldn't stop. Hal Eiseley was very embarrassed and Dr. Foxx was clearly furious, but she could not stop; it was the most terrible thing. Russian vodka on top of too many Dexamyls was probably all it was, or perhaps the strain of not showing what she felt was beginning to show, but it could have been just seeing old Hal Eiseley, who had been so positive she was going to grow up to be a terrific writer some day and she hadn't.

Hal Eiseley and Dr. Foxx made a lot of polite embarrassed noises, and scrambled around paying checks and collecting stuff to get her out of there because people were staring at them, and just before they reached the door Hal Eiseley put his arm around her shoulder and said very quietly, "You're beautiful and talented, you know; you always were."

Which of course made her cry even harder. He

was an extraordinarily nice man, and extraordinary niceness in a man was one of those things she couldn't handle. Then he said it again, in her ear, pressing her shoulder one last time as Dr. Foxx steered her out the door in the Ukrainian peasant woman's apron. "Beautiful and talented," Hal whispered, pressing her shoulder, as if he were pressing two gold coins in her hand, coins in some foreign currency, Ukrainian probably, that had no exchange rate at the hotel where she was staying with Dr. Foxx.

When they got there and she had stopped sobbing long enough to stammer how sorry she was about making such a terrible scene and spoiling everything, she noticed he was very pale and probably more upset than she was. "Why the hell did you have to do that?" he shouted at her in a frightening voice. And "What kind of a bastard did you want that man to think I was? Was that the point? Well, was it? Answer me, damn you!"

She didn't know, she didn't have any point, she hadn't meant, but she couldn't speak at all; her throat was apparently closed for emergency repairs, due to some sort of mechanical breakdown.

"For God's sake," he demanded, and now she was sure he would strike her, such a rage it was. "What the hell do you *want* from me!"

"Nothing," she finally whispered through the searing pain in her throat. "Oh, God, I swear, nothing."

Then he looked at her so coldly that she could feel the death of whatever there had been. As if he

139

could kill her, if only that were not exactly what she wished he would do. It was; they both knew that. It would have been her final wish in the wishing well in the small hotel, but there wasn't one, was there? And her wishing he would kill her, she was almost sure, was why he stormed out of the room instead, leaving her alone in the strange not-quite-miraculous foreign city. He had to leave her there, just like that, with her very last wish as unfulfilled as all the others.

It seemed reasonable to assume that he would not leave for home without his new attaché case that had his appointment book in it. And he would not have left the wallet or the bottle of Meprobamate on the dresser, or, for that matter, the knit blazer that she had just bought him. Did he think she was going to pack up all his stuff and take it home for him, as well as pay the hotel bill? Not that she wouldn't. Maybe he knew her too well?

Well, then, was she just going to go on lying here on this tear-sodden bedspread until he came back? Is that what he thought? Would she consider swallowing all the Meprobamate? She had a brief, thoroughly satisfying vision of his face over that one. Suicide, she had long known, might be the ultimate masochism, but it was also the ultimate sadism. And what if he were less sorry about losing her than about being stranded up here without a single sleeping pill? What if that made him even angrier at her than he already was, and not sorry at all? She would much prefer being carted off to whatever passed for Bellevue in Vancouver, where they would discover that she had been transformed into a hopeless, raving schizophrenic. I am dead but still watching you from inside this other maniac self. Crazy, ha-ha, I'll show you crazy. EX-PATIENT CRACKS IN PSYCHIATRIST'S HOTEL ROOM. BLAMES HIM.

Besides, if he turned out to be really sorry, if it made him realize suddenly what a fool he had been and how much he'd loved her all along if only he'd stopped to think, she could always recover and forgive him. Whereas with suicide, she wouldn't be leaving him with much hope for a possible reconciliation.

Attempted suicide—now, maybe that was a viable compromise. Not *too* dead. But she wasn't much of a judge about dosages. For instance, she had no idea how much Dexamyl she had taken today. A lot, was about as close as she could estimate, considering her crazy reaction at the Russian pavilion, plus the vodka—two of them—and now those unmarked big white pills of his. God knew how many milligrams they tucked into one of those; he never took more than a half, which was usually enough to knock him out for seven hours. One whole one? Better not, she thought. One whole one might get her right past "attempted" and onto a slab at the Vancouver morgue, without so much as page 27 written in her first book; no one could publish *that* unfinished a novel. So much for Hal Eiseley and his crystal ball, and they'd have to get her parents to fly up here in the middle of the school term all the way from Ann

Arbor, when her mother was terrified of flying and her father was on digitalis.

All things considered, "attempted" seemed risky. She decided to pack everything first, pay the whole bill and check out, leaving him a terse, ambiguous note. Then, after packing, she looked in the mirror at her puffy eyes and decided on no note at all. The least he could do was worry. She left his attaché case with the room clerk, but she took his knit blazer because it smelled of him, and also the bottle of Meprobamate because maybe she would change her mind and want to do that other thing, and it was smart to keep all your options.

Then she took a taxi to Hal Eiseley's hotel and left a message at the desk that she was in the bar and wondered if he had time for a farewell drink with an old newspaper buddy. After an hour or so he came, and they had four farewell drinks and she had another good cry, and then they went up to his room, where he kissed her and said, "God, I wanted to do this with you for so long, so long . . ." And she thought, So long at the fair.

Suddenly she wanted a bath, she who never wanted a bath, and he ran it for her and soaped her slowly and tenderly, her breasts and her thighs, leaning over the side of the tub, and then she got out and he rubbed her dry with a big hotel towel and then with his tongue like a mother cat, and he said, "Kissing you here is exactly like kissing you there. Exactly." And she went to sleep in his big bed, in his big arms, and it was nice.

The next day Hal drove her to the airport and

she blew him a kiss through the plane window and he saluted her. She could see his lips forming the magic words one last time: "Beautiful and talented." She sighed. Nice.

Chapter

TEN

"NICE," SIGHED SOPHY, dreamily licking a chickeny finger. "Now, that kind of man could be the answer for everybody."

She laughed. "Not for his wife, I don't think." Then she added soberly, "Not for me, either. I mean, a good sudsy screw is one thing—"

"Yeah," Sophy agreed passionately.

"—but a sex *life* is something else."

"Maybe it's supposed to be that way," mused Tess. "Maybe if God meant for us to screw one person throughout our entire sex lives, he'd have—"

"*He?*" exclaimed Laurie, giggling.

Tess ignored that. "—have given us shorter sex lives."

"Yes," she said. "Well."

Wanda got up off the couch and stretched out on the floor pillows; she always did that when she had a serious announcement. They gazed down at her expectantly. She closed her eyes. "Your turn, Wanda," prompted Laurie.

"What's the topic?" she asked, not bothering to open her eyes.

"Sex versus love," Tess replied irritably. "Sort of."

"Mmm," said Wanda listlessly. "Well, I don't believe in either of those any more. I've got a whole new philosophy that doesn't include those at all."

"How does Stanley like it?" said Sophy. Stanley was Wanda's husband of seven lean years, and also of seven fat—which is to say that he was mostly overweight and underpaid, during the same seven years.

"Stanley," said Wanda defensively, "is coming along fine."

The new philosophy, she told them finally—with some reluctance, though possibly she only wanted to seem reluctant—rested on a simple basic concept which she had named "the good part." Wanda had been working on the good part for the past five months, ever since the awful night when Stanley woke her up at three-thirty A.M. by yelling in her ear, "When do we get to the *good* part?" And she had shaken him off groggily, mumbling, "Good part? We already *had* the good part." Stanley rolled over and started to cry like a great heaving baby, loud enough to wake up their two children, their pregnant Doberman pinscher and the civil rights activist who lived downstairs. Fat, loving Stanley, his grief shaking the loft bed he had just built them. Finally she had reached over and hugged him and promised to try to think of something.

She had lain awake thinking for the rest of that night, she told them, and at about six-fifteen it came to her—the idea of the good part. She looked over at Stanley's big woolly body lying there like a stuffed teddy from F.A.O. Schwarz and decided to try using it. Like any other sexual toy, just for fun. Just the way she had decided one day to try the Scoopmaster ice-cream scoop in her kitchen drawer, having noticed suddenly that it had this nice smooth enamel handle with shallow curved ridges all around. It turned out to be nicely weighted, so that after you slipped the handle gently inside all the way, the scoop part would balance itself without tipping, thereby freeing both your hands in case you needed them for anything else. Wanda was very high on the Scoopmaster.

One of the first things she tried under "the good part" was showing Stanley how she used the Scoopmaster. An object lesson, she called it. She said it took her less than a minute to have the most terrific orgasm with the Scoopmaster, right in front of Stanley. And in that one single minute, she said, Stanley had learned more than he had ever picked up on his own in the seven years they had been fucking in the dark.

After that, Wanda said, it was really easy. She opened all the kitchen drawers and took out several other nice things with interesting handles, and she bought a battery vibrator and musk oil and a penis-numbing cream called De-Tane, and some well-shaped cucumbers at two for thirty-nine, and they went to work. They tried all kinds of dumb movements and positions, and she had her first anal orgasm, which she said was not in the least degrading if you didn't *think* it was in the least degrading and all in all, life had picked up quite a lot in the last five months. The good part, Wanda said, was probably the greatest sexual discovery since Masters and Johnson found the preorgasmic mucosa flush—or maybe since the first vestal virgin snuffed out her votive candle and found something that worked in more wondrous ways than God.

"Amen," said Sophy fervently, and they all forced little laughs to ward off any lurking demons.

Dr. Foxx was having trouble getting through to John Murdock. He had left three increasingly urgent messages with what sounded like three separate secretaries. He had also called Murdock's home and left messages with the maid—maids?—and wife, who, he assumed, was still Diane. So far Murdock had not returned a single call.

Foxx was understandably distraught—sick, in fact. His eyes cast mournful shadows like the badges of an outclassed fighter, and the ghastly pallor under his tan had turned his face the color of advanced hepatitis. He had not slept since Vancouver, four full nights, had now misplaced every valuable document pertaining to any phase of his life, and was driving around carrying the crumpled stubs of his license and registration, clearly stamped "NOT A LI-

CENSE" and "NOT A VALID REGISTRATION," respectively.

By a supreme effort of will, he was still functioning with his patients. A talented therapist can do that, the way an expert pilot can fly on perfectly tuned instruments. In some ways, the worse Foxx felt, the better he did with his patients; all their terrors reflected and pulled at his own, as in a hall of distorting mirrors. One patient, a boy of fifteen, had once remarked that Foxx had the face of a person whose lifelong ambition was to be a tortured saint, provided he could do his own torturing. Like most psychotics, the boy had an uncanny sense of truth, as opposed to reality.

He had not heard from her, either, since the afternoon she fled from their hotel with all his sleeping pills. It was *her* fault he hadn't slept all week. He could have gotten more pills if he knew where his prescription pads were. Damn her. He knew she was all right, so it was safe to curse her. He had called *Penchants* and identified himself as a Futuro public relations man with some follow-up information for her story on the fair. One of the editors told him she was in town, and had called in but wasn't expected in the office until late Tuesday. Foxx left his name and number. Of course, it was possible no one had given her the message. Unlike Murdock.

On Thursday night he took the last tuna pie out of his freezer and the last fourteen string beans out of his fresh-vegetable bin. He had bought the beans two weeks ago in the country; by his standards they were still fresh. He never bought vegetables frozen or canned. He loved keeping track of produce prices; finding a stand on the highway with beans for twenty-nine cents a pound was almost like winning a tennis match in straight sets. He would stand jubilantly over his rickety kitchen table, lining up three or four beans at a time, snapping off their crisp little ends with professional barber's shears, so that there was very little waste. He always made an elaborate salad as well, even if the lettuce had wilted into the fragile softness of aged skin, even if the tomatoes, cruelly reddened by gas injections, had the taste of wet sand. He made his own classic French dressing, discarding only the merest white fibrous tips of the scallions, slicing radishes thin enough to read through. For these few minutes, laboring over his dinner, inhaling his warming tuna pie as it mingled with the fragrant ghosts of spills from other well-remembered solitary meals, he could almost forget how miserable he was, and how alone.

He was cleaning the foil pie plate (he always saved these; he had enough foil pie plates to serve a hundred people, if he should ever want to feed a hundred people off reused, slightly grease-filmed foil pie plates) when the phone rang. It was Murdock —jovial, light-voiced Murdock—returning his call. Foxx refrained from asking which call. How were things going, he asked. He had just been wondering, not having heard from John since he had signed over his life and all that money. He tried to sound jovial too, and failed miserably.

Oh, splendid, truly splendid was how things were going. Murdock's voice was fairly bursting with glib tidings about his latest scouting trip in the Caribbean, looking over territory for the second tennis resort—T/C/2, as he called it. Right now it looked like the ball would go to St. Maartens or one of the British Virgins. He would know in another week; he'd give Foxx a call on it; he was making a note right now to do that; he could certainly understand Foxx's interest; in fact, he appreciated it; so few people, even *major* investors (he let that one drop very lightly), showed any kind of genuine interest in the process of setting up a complicated project like this.

Foxx just wanted to mention, by the way, that his accountant hadn't been able to get Murdock's accountant on the phone, for some reason, and that he had called partly to ask if Murdock would mind asking his accountant to let Foxx's accountant check some figures that Foxx's accountant seemed to be having some trouble adding up.

Murdock wondered politely if Foxx's accountant might be an utter incompetent, since the figures were all very clear. To illustrate, he threw a number of clear figures in the air, caught them deftly and added them up, or said he did, and then pointed out that any reasonably bright seventh-grader should be able to come up with the same answer, he would have thought. Oh, and he'd be glad to recommend a really topnotch man to Foxx if he was considering firing his accountant.

He had to run now, but why didn't Foxx pop over for dinner tomorrow night. He could bring any-one he liked, of course; the occasion was just that

Murdock had brought Diane a marvelous pasta-making machine from Italy a week ago. He was thinking of investing in the company that made these; in fact, he was flying over again next week with some of his people to check out the firm's management. He had a feeling that American health nuts were ripe for homemade pasta equipment; yogurt makers and juice extractors had paved the way, after all. In any case, they were planning to try out the machine tomorrow; he'd asked a few other folks and it should be some species of fun, no? And perhaps they could talk more then. About business.

By the time Murdock hung up, Foxx felt markedly worse. Murdock was undoubtedly lying; the figures he had jotted down while Murdock was tossing them out made no sense whatever, but his own accountant probably *was* incompetent. Why the hell else couldn't he get Murdock's accountant on the phone?

He took half a Dexedrine in order to stay up and worry more alertly, washed it down with his last slice of two-week-old apple pie from the A&P, only slightly green, and rinsed the foil pan to add it to his collection. Then he decided to call someone to take to Murdock's tomorrow night. He had to use the big telephone book, because God knew where his little blue one was and he was in no mood to deal with the furies at Information. He called the brunette Jean and the blond Jean, and Iris the stewardess, and Mitzi who had just landed the lead in a new road-company production of *Mame*, and Terry who made seventy-five dollars an hour modeling just her hands. He hadn't seen any of them for months, and they all sounded busy or married or unpleasantly cool, except for Iris the stewardess' roommate, whom he had never met. So finally he gave up and threw the phone book into the mess on the floor, which was when she called.

She had not received any message from him at *Penchants*, she said. "How are you, anyway," she said.

"Fair," he said. Followed by silence.

"I—" she began.

"I—" he said, colliding with hers. "I'm sorry about —" he tried then.

"Don't," she cut in quickly.

He could feel the first tears welling in her eyes. "Would you like to see me tomorrow?" he asked, delivering it lightly to brush the saltwater out of her voice.

She drew in a breath—sharp, audible, like an inverted sigh. "Why?" she asked. "Do you want to see *me*?"

"Sure." He admitted it, straight out—well, almost straight. "Sure" was, after all, less committal than "yes." One could toss off, or away, any number of "sures" without meaning "yes." "John Murdock invited us to dinner," he said, signifying that had John Murdock not invited them, then perhaps not even the "sure" would apply.

"Us?" she said.

"Well, me. And whoever."

"Whoever," she echoed, which made him squirm, and now he wanted very much to hang up. Now breathing was hard for *him*. "I have to go," he said,

153

trying to sound vaguely rushed. "Seven all right, tomorrow?"

"Seven tomorrow," she echoed tonelessly. Someone—whoever—would be all right at seven tomorrow. "Sure."

There were fifty people at the Murdocks', and Diane, lightly dusted with flour, never did come out of the kitchen. John held court in the library, the only finished room of their twelve-room penthouse, which they'd been camping in for two years because Diane couldn't find a decorator she could stand. A few pieces of furniture covered in muslin, with swatches of fifty-dollar-a-yard imported damasks pinned to them, stood around pending decision, surrounded by vast space, beautiful paneling, crystal chandeliers and, of course, the aquaria. Only the built-in closets had ever been completed—by the previous tenant. Diane was considering ripping all the drawers out, along with their antique ivory knobs, but then there would be no place to put their clothes, so she and John and the children and the fish were making do with just the paneling, chandeliers and the really tacky closets until she could find some faggot it was possible to work with. So far she had fired nine.

From seven-thirty until ten forty-five Murdock poured drinks and excellent wine, opened tins of foie gras and piled sour cream and caviar into giant raw mushrooms. Those who were unavoidably getting drunk occasionally wandered out to the kitchen to see Diane and the celebrated pasta machine. They were both there, all right, Diane rolling doughy moun-

154

tains like a nursery-school sculptor gone mad, and the machine, all silver and bristling with red knobs, towering above a new Carrara marble peninsula fitted with outlets, warming trays and pop-out built-in toasters and sliding partitions for cooling and warming things, and storage drawers for twenty-four separate parts of blenders, mixers and crushers. Diane was forcing the doughy mountains into the pasta machine and cranking spigots. Sure enough, the mountains subsided within, and out the other end came a painfully thin continuous strand of noodle. Judging from the size of the mountain and the speed with which the noodle issued forth, it would be Tuesday before dinner was served.

At eleven o'clock Murdock himself went out to the kitchen, glanced at his finely dusted wife with wordless contempt, armed himself with several chilled bottles of Moët & Chandon, a fresh kilo of Beluga, several jars of macadamia nuts, more sour cream and baby pickled corn and pâté and sour cream, and stormed back to the library, pausing briefly at the swinging kitchen door to snarl, "You've proved your point, cunt. Now call somebody and get us some food."

Diane blinked her floury eyes, wiped her hands on her red-checked apron that said "Don't Kiss Me I'm Cooking," and left via the rear kitchen door which led to the service elevator. Murdock himself called a neighborhood Italian restaurant, which he said had rated four stars and three triangles in *The New York Times,* and ordered a ton of gluey spaghetti that could not possibly have come from cans marked

Franco-American, though one wondered. Several guests spilled orange blobs on the muslin-covered sofas that were going back to the last decorator next week. There was witty conversation and the tinkling of real nine-millimeter pearls against Steuben stemware, and clever men in black silk turtleneck shirts, looking like futuristic space explorers on Channel 9, talked about what a shame it was that Murdock had been shafted by the Sudanese in that oil business. Casually Foxx asked one of the clever men what it was all about. The Sudanese had nationalized their oil just when John was about to make a killing on it, the man explained. Blew the whole fucking deal. Damn shame.

It was the following Thursday before Foxx heard that on Monday Diane Murdock had filed for divorce and that John Murdock had filed simultaneously for bankruptcy. Diane, it seemed, was now considering suing all of John's limited partners in Tennis/Carib because John claimed to be flat broke, even though he had moved into a magnificent, fully furnished apartment and was still riding around town in a company limousine, and all Diane had in the house to feed the children was champagne, baby pickled corn and the ingredients for a lifetime supply of homemade noodles.

John himself called Foxx to commiserate. "Got a little too far ahead of ourselves with the expansion" was how he put it. He had filed for bankruptcy, he explained, "just to protect ourselves." But he saw no need for Foxx to worry. "Once we've worked out all the figures," he said airily, "I think we'll find that with the losses, taxwise we may actually come out ahead for the year."

"Oh," said Foxx. "Well, that's a relief."

"Oh, and let me know if you want the name of that accountant," said Murdock. Click.

Phrases he had heard the night of the noodle party wafted back into his throbbing head. "Leased some computers from IBM . . ." ". . . extra staff to keep on top of the new business . . ." ". . . new suite in the Trade Center . . ." ". . . commissioned a sculpture for the reception room . . ." ". . . scouting trips . . ." ". . . Sudanese oil . . ." He closed his eyes and saw Murdock in his limousine, sipping Moët & Chandon. He heard Murdock's silky voice again in his ear: ". . . with the losses, taxwise we may actually come out ahead . . ." He smiled painfully, wondering who the "we" might be. John and his rare neon tetra? Unless Diane had already drained the water out of the tanks and fed the piranha to the children—or vice versa.

He had shifted all his Friday appointments around to arrange a three-day weekend, but after Murdock's call on Thursday he had scarcely moved out of his chair. He gazed feebly out the window, like an invalid, telling time only by the growth of his whiskers, ignoring his tiredness. It was too much trouble to shift to the bed, even; if he dozed here, sitting up—what difference? He let the answering machine pick up the calls; he did not even bother to flick the switch to find out what new disasters might have befallen him. There came a point when it seemed better not to know.

Late on Friday afternoon she appeared at his door with a suitcase. She looked frightened; it didn't occur to him that he was frightening to look at. "Your message on the machine," she stammered, staring at his sleepless gray unshaven face, his matted hair. "It didn't make sense. I mean, I knew you were here. I thought . . . you said—"

He tried to summon a coherent reply. "I can't," he said, frowning and waving her away.

"Can't what?" she demanded, following him in with the suitcase, picking her way through the scattered mail. The room looked as ransacked as he did: papers strewn on every surface, including the floor; more papers piled on every chair but his. Only a mad burglar could have wreaked such chaos in a single day, or Dr. Foxx himself in a state of advanced shock. She moved things, sat on the floor in front of him, took both his cold hands and squeezed them. "What happened?" she commanded. "I'm not moving until you tell me."

He sighed. "Tell you," he echoed. "I have been wiped out. Financially. I have lost all my money. *All.* I have even lost ten thousand dollars of *borrowed* money. I actually borrowed ten thousand dollars to give him, see, and that's gone too."

"To give . . . John Murdock?" she asked gently.

His eyes opened slightly, indicating that she had guessed right.

"And he—"

Foxx shrugged. "Murdock's firm is bankrupt. Murdock himself is probably swell—taxwise." He told her briefly about Tennis/Carib, as much as he could bear telling. Even that was too much. When he finished, she picked up his phone.

"What are you doing?"

"Canceling my trip, obviously."

He remembered something about her flying to London tonight; hence the suitcase. "Why bother?" he said dully.

"Something came up," she said softly, smoothing his hair. "Down, I mean. I have this emergency. I have to visit this doctor here for a few days."

He closed his eyes wearily. Distantly he heard her explaining to *Penchants* about her "emergency." She could reschedule the trip next week if they could arrange it with the girl rock singers she was being sent to interview. They could get in touch with her here; she gave them his number.

"Now," she said brightly, "hot bath. Food?" She looked doubtfully toward his kitchen. "Anything in there to eat?"

"Ashes," he said.

She ran the bath and then bustled out to the kitchen.

"Goddamn nurse," he bellowed. "Leave me alone. My life is over."

"Bulldickey," she said snippily, unbuttoning his shirt. "Get in there and wash. You are a piggy person."

He laughed and was startled to find that it hurt. "It hurts when I laugh," he yelled at her mournfully.

"Who asked you to laugh?" she yelled back. "Cry! You just lost all your money!"

"Bitch!" he yelled.

"Financial wizard!" she shrieked. "Conglomera-teur!"

She was scrambling eggs and making coffee; it smelled good. He wallowed in the tubwater and self-pity until she came in, yanked the plug, pulled him out and bundled him into the terry-cloth robe she had bought him in Vancouver because she was embarrassed when he answered their hotel room door in his raincoat.

"Why do you waste your youth on a broken failure of a man, a pauper? My grandmother said it was just as easy to love a rich person. She had Gloria Vanderbilt in mind for me."

"Wow, is that lucky," she said. "If your grand-mother had had her way, Gloria Vanderbilt might be flat broke tonight. Put on your slippers."

He shuffled meekly after her into the kitchen and wolfed her eggs and coffee in silence, like a disaster victim accepting a handout from the Red Cross.

Penchants called back and said the London in-terview was set for a week from Monday, and they hoped she felt better.

"Oh, I have the utmost faith in this doctor," she said. "He's a wizard."

"Fuck you," said Foxx after she hung up.

"Possibly later," she replied, kissing him. "But now let's just lie in the bed and talk. I'd like to hear your side of it."

"Of what?"

"Your grandmother."

"My grandmother," he began obediently, following her to the bedroom, "used to feel the fat pads on my fingers to see if I'd gained enough weight."

"Mmm," she said. "Like the witch in *Hansel and Gretel.*" She handed him the clothes that were piled on the bed. "Hang up," she said.

"Why did she?" he asked, halfway to the closet.

"Who?"

"The witch."

"Oh. To see if Hansel was fat enough to be eaten yet. Gretel kept fooling her by sticking a chicken bone through the cage bars. I never understood where the chicken came from."

"The egg," he said, and burst into uncontrollable laughter.

"Overtired," she observed, patting the bed. "Get in."

"Bossy," he retorted. "I never nap in the daytime." But he got in, sighing deeply, and she did too, even though it was light out and scarcely six o'clock, and she rubbed his back and he talked. Endlessly, as if she had switched him on somehow, the child in him, the lostness.

He had never belonged to his grandmother. Never belonged. She didn't even have the sense to talk to him in Hungarian; she spoke broken English to him. "And she cooked vegetables to death. No salad. Bone marrow, she fed me—dug it out of the bone and fed it to me with a spoon."

"Did you like it?"

"I don't remember. She said I couldn't whistle because I didn't eat my carrots. Not true."

"Can you whistle now?"

"Sure." He blew faintly and fell asleep trying.

"Eat your carrots," she whispered, kissing the back of his neck. She dozed too, until he stirred, mumbling again. "They lied to the Board of Education," he said.

"Mmm?"

"Said I lived with my great-aunt on 84th Street; so I could go to P.S. 6. Never lived with my aunt. Lived in a slum railroad flat on 101st Street. Never could bring anyone home from school. Always outside. Always ashamed."

"I love you," she said, but he was asleep again.

Fitfully he woke and told about the eggnog line in camp for the puny kids. About his stepfather who never touched him. Never kissed, never hit, never hugged. About how they got him a scholarship to Williston Prep, the only white middle-class boy in the school on scholarship.

"There must have been other kids on scholarship," she said.

"All Indians," he said, dozing off.

"Forrest Grunewald," he muttered the next time he came to.

"Mmm?"

"Lived on Park Avenue. They all did. Took me home once. His parents had Italian chocolates in the living room. 'You can take two,' Forrest said. 'My parents count them every night.'" He began to laugh again, wildly, and just as it turned into a sob he shuddered and was silent. She held him tight and said "Ssh" and "I love you" until his breathing settled into a peaceful rhythm.

Later, when he had slept for hours, he told her
that he had never had a room of his own anywhere.
Sleeping on the living-room sofa at his grandmother's
house. Never bringing a child home all through Williston Prep. Then one day he did, for some reason. Later
he told his mother—who lived in a nice clean mid-
town apartment—about it, and she was horrified.
"Why didn't you bring the boy *here?*" she said. "But
I don't have a room here," he explained. "You can't
bring a kid home and when he asks where's your
room, where's your stuff, you have no place to show
him."

His mother and stepfather did take him in, finally, when he was sixteen and on the verge of leaving
for college. His mother said it wasn't nice for a college boy to go on living in a slum with an illiterate
Hungarian grandmother. "When my mother died," he
went on, "my stepfather thought it would be best if
we called it a day too. That's what he said; we should
'terminate the relationship,' he said."

"How old were you?"

"Twenty. I was in the Army. At twenty it was
official that nobody ever loved me."

"What about your grandmother?" she said. "With
the bone marrow?"

He smiled. "Maybe she did. She said if only I
smiled, the whole world would belong to me, including Gloria Vanderbilt. Didn't tell John Murdock,
though. Wonder if I should call him back about that."

"Mmm," she said. "Ssh."

She asked him if he thought his mother died of
guilt.

"No," he said. "Cancer."

"Cancer *caused* by guilt, I mean. I have this theory. People who die young of cancer are riddled with guilt first."

"You should have been dead years ago, then," he said.

"Not *my* kind of guilt. Not nameless, all-purpose dumb guilt. *Real* guilt—for genuine crimes."

"My mother was never convicted."

"Yes, but she abandoned you. She married a man who wouldn't even *pretend* he didn't hate you. Do you look like your real father? I bet you do. *Do* you?"

"Spitting image," he said. "That's why my real father abandoned me on the occasion of my birth."

"Mmm," she said. "See?"

"Sure," he said. "How about we screw now?"

"Mmm," she said, smiling. "I thought he'd never get to that part."

It was nearly five A.M. then, and they were both far too exhausted to do much more than nuzzle like tired children, licking and stroking and dropping off midstroke, each trying to curl up inside the other somehow, as if for safekeeping. Finally they found a way to close all the spaces tightly, like interlocking puzzle pieces.

Chapter

ELEVEN

THEY SPENT THE weekend like lovers, hugging and laughing and grinning sheepishly at each other. She helped him clean up; every time one of them found something—his license, his address book, his overdue Con Ed bill—Foxx would hold it aloft like a holy object and cry reverently, "An omen!" They made a treasure hunt of it. She found his car key in a shoe under the bed—and that was when she discovered his real buried treasure: Army footlockers filled with hoarded souvenirs from every trip he had ever taken anywhere. Duty-free bottles of expensive brandy; sealed boxes of famous perfumes; gold-threaded Indian saris wrapped in dusty cellophane, filthy and discolored from years of disuse; hideous tiny porcelain mice nibbling minute chunks of porcelain cheese; ancient crazed pottery bearing hieroglyphics that probably said "Fuck Tourism"; temple rubbings; brass elephants; maps of downtown Rome as it looked in 1955; antique *Guides Michelin* showing the best twenty-year-old routes to every fine restaurant in the French provinces, all of which had long since closed or passed on to children who couldn't cook a decent cassoulet to save their stars.

He grinned at her, blushing, as she dug down through his years. "Now you know everything," he said.

"I *already* knew," she said.

"But not how *bad*," he protested.

"Oh, I had an inkling," she said, "from the foil pie plates. Also the brown grocery bags. You know," she added thoughtfully, "if all else fails you could open an airport shop."

"That's not funny," he said. "Those happen to be extremely valuable—*everything* in there."

She held up the small porcelain mouse wordlessly.

"Fifteen dollars at Georg Jensen, if you want to know," he said, and marched out of the room, clearly hurt.

"Hey," she said, following him. "They're very nice, each in its own way. Do you hang on to people like that?"

He nodded gravely. "Never use *them*, either. Just save them. I go to Williston Prep reunions."

"Not on scholarship, though."

He smiled. "I also keep in touch with old girl friends."

"Do they like that?"

"Sure. Wouldn't you?"

"No," she said seriously.

"Well, they never forget old Foxxy. I'm the one who taught them all to brush after every meal. Kicked them out of bed if they forgot."

"If you're such a health nut, how come you take all those pills?" she asked. She had just picked four assorted halves out of his pajama pocket, and a crumbled Dexie mixed with fuzz out of the shirt he'd worn yesterday.

"I'm only a health nut about things I'm afraid of. I'm afraid of losing my teeth. I couldn't stand being an old man with no lips. Lyndon Johnson had no lips before he died."

"What if I told you that Lyndon Johnson brushed after every meal, but took Dexies to wake up and Miltowns to sleep?"

"I'd say he should have cut down to *half* a pill at a time. He might still be dead, but maybe he'd have gone in a better mood."

"Crazy," she said.

"Takes one . . ." he murmured, and hugged her lightly.

He cooked her a steak and she cooked him an omelet, and on Saturday night she got him to go to bed without his *APA News*. On Sunday they went for a walk on the Lower East Side, where he taught her how to comparison-shop for fruits and vegetables. It took them two hours to cover the twenty-eight stands between 5th and 15th streets, buying scallions, kohlrabi and beets with the tops on (*two* vegetables for the price of one!) and they only got stuck once. They fell for the bananas at twelve cents a pound, only to find them two blocks north for eleven, but by that time he felt so good that he almost didn't care.

When they went to bed on Sunday he set the alarm for seven-fifteen. He had a seven-thirty patient. Neither of them mentioned the possibility of her leaving. She had never slept there overnight, into patient hours; she wondered if he had thought about it. She woke up at five and lay awake worrying until the alarm went off. He silenced it at once, and leaned over to make sure it hadn't disturbed her. She pretended to be asleep; he kissed her hair, got out of bed carefully, so as not to jostle her, and left.

He was only a room away, but she felt as if he had shut all the old doors. *He* had been able to leave, but *she* had not. Trapped, she thought; I'm a shut-in. Today we will play a special song for our shut-ins. Tony Bennett sings "I need no shackles to remind me . . ." She thought of her old fantasy about emerging every hour to service him. No ruffled apron, but perhaps she could make one out of an old bedsheet.

Instead she started to clean the bedroom. Then the bathroom. On your knees, atta girl, she thought grimly; shake that can. Jennifer Jones was scrubbing the floor when Gregory Peck raped her in *Duel in the Sun,* which she had seen four times. The telephone rang twice; she shuddered. It was not for her; it could not be for her. This was Dr. Foxx's office, and nobody calls the maid, not even if she's Jennifer Jones.

Then she tried *not* to clean. She picked up the book that she had bought to read on the plane to London. She opened it to page one and fastened her eyes on the first word, "Somewhere," until it looked silly, a process that took fifteen seconds. Then she closed the book and stared into the mirror until she found the lines she was looking for. She made a series of ugly faces of the kind her mother said would freeze that way, and then cleaned the mirror. Now the lines looked like deep folds. See what you get?

She went through his bureau drawers. No pictures of nuns. She dove back into the musty treasures in his footlockers. She shook one of the ancient bottles of Chanel Number 5; there was no sound of fluid. Three hundred dollars' worth of fancy French perfume must have evaporated inside all those sealed packages; whom had he bought it for? She examined the saris, the cheap Mexican serapes, the braided belts and the straw mats. She pictured him standing on dusty brown streets bargaining with dusty brown natives. How much if I take all? We round it off, yes? I take all you got, these, and those, and those too—one hundred drachma for all, yes? She pictured the dusty brown native smiling broadly. Foxx drove a hard bargain only on string beans.

She pressed her ear to the wall. Perhaps he was revealing the secret of life to someone else. Nothing. She sighed. What if he came back and found her eavesdropping instead of cleaning? No, wait a minute; he hadn't told her to stay back here all day long, shuffling silently among his souvenirs. What *did* he expect her to be doing? Leaving, probably. That was it; he thought she was gone by now.

Panic seized her; she swallowed hard, like a passenger on the wrong express elevator shooting past her floor. That *was* it, of course; she had no *business* here. He was inside *functioning* at his work, wasn't he? Whereas the minute he left her, *she had ceased to have any function at all.*

But where could she go? What function *could* she serve? She stood there, desperate and helpless, like a lost child in a department store. Shopping? Yes! She could go to the supermarket *for him.* She could buy things to cook, perchance to clean, *for him.* She could get another can of Ajax.

First, though, she would need—she searched distractedly through his top drawer—Dexedrine! She took two whole ones and broke two others in half so that the bottle would appear as full as he remembered. Not that he ever remembered anything like that, but just in case. Then she scribbled a note— "Gone shopping!"—and laid it on the pillow. Taking his key, she tiptoed out, not daring to breathe, past his door like a terrified naughty child, though he had said not to worry about keeping quiet. Sometimes, he pointed out, his cleaning woman worked in the other rooms while he had patients. He was not a Freudian, he didn't need total silence, and neither did his patients. Still, she would not breathe. She carried her shoes to put them on in the hall outside. Then she remembered that she would have to pass the waiting room. Did he have an eight-fifteen patient? She couldn't remember. What if someone were sitting there, reading *Esquire,* and she tiptoed out like this, carrying her shoes? Would the person assume she was a patient leaving? Barefoot? She stopped, put on her shoes and tried to muster a dignified patient-look. I'm not sick; I'm just passing through. It was the effect she had always striven for when she *was his* patient.

For the first half-hour in the supermarket she was happy. She hummed with the Muzak, filling her cart like all the normal ladies she passed in the aisles. She could make a roast lamb just like they did. Did he like roast lamb? She had already piled the lamb, applesauce, potatoes, mint jelly and spices into the cart before the question occurred to her. Maybe she should ask him first? Call him from here, in the middle of a patient hour? Take it home and freeze it if he didn't like it? Every possibility sounded crazy. She wheeled the cart around and started putting everything back methodically, in its proper place. Then she started over. She started over three different times, filling the cart and emptying it, until she felt the cold sweat gathering and knew that she had to get out of there. Hamburger was safe. She loaded up one last time, fighting the sweat and panic. She sagged against the check-out counter, breathing deep. "You all right?" the clerk asked. "Sure," she said. "Except I forgot the Ajax." "Jesus," said the clerk, irritated now. "I got three people waiting; I'm the only one open here." "I'm sorry," she gasped, "I'll go to the end of the line." "I already *checked* this stuff, lady," he snarled. "Okay," she said meekly, "I'll skip the Ajax." Meaning that she would stop in another supermarket for it. She could not go back without Ajax; she had no plans for the rest of the day that did not include Ajax.

She did better in the second supermarket. She was more confident now, with two full bags. See how I can shop? she thought. I can carry *four* bags; I can even stop at the bakery and get a pie; he likes pie; I can carry the pie box by the string in my teeth. Recklessly she decided to buy the lamb roast, plus accessories. She had to quit now, or it would take two trips to get the stuff back to his house. Not that she minded making two trips; after all, what else did she have to do? It was the doorman; she didn't want the doorman to see her that many times with that many bags. Something crazy about that woman, he'd say; Dr. Foxx sure gets some doozies.

She made it back to the house, staggering, just in time. The bottom paper bag was tearing; she could hear the insidious sound all the way down the block. They always put the cans on the bottom, so that the sharp edges pierce right through the paper. They like to see women picking up dented cans from the sidewalk, she thought. Splattered eggs are even better. It's a form of sadism you rarely read about, but that's because they've hushed it up. Next time your bag tears, spilling your entire life in the street, look back at the supermarket window and count the grinning faces; you'll see.

Struggling up the four steps to his apartment, trying desperately not to rattle the bags (the pie

172

box *was* in her teeth; there was no other way to manage the key) she thought, Oh, I am a beast of intolerable burden; Oh, I am an intolerable beast. Not breathing was very hard by now.

The patient who was leaving bumped smack into her, of course, just as the next patient arrived. Right after the crash, Dr. Foxx appeared, scowling. At least she saw it as scowling. As she saw it, he stared at her in murderous silence, and then retreated inside, followed by the new patient, who kept looking back over his shoulder. There were searing pains in her wrists and groin. She could not move; she stood paralyzed on his doorstep that she had sullied with broken eggs and leaking blood from the lamb. Possibly the Angel of Death would pass over this night and spare his firstborn. Then Dr. Foxx might forgive her. Otherwise there was nothing she could do to undo what she had done. *Nothing.* He had made a mistake, letting her stay. That was all.

She spent the rest of the day in an orgy of remorse and atonement, consisting of equal parts tears and detergent suds. She sponged everything spongeable; everything else she wiped dry. She even polished his dusty shoes. His cleaning lady would not have to come this week; indeed, if she could hermetically seal the place, no cleaning lady would ever have to come again. She had saved him at least ten dollars plus carfare. That was something, anyway. She did not care to think what, exactly.

She unpacked all the food without crackling the paper bags, a feat which took her nearly an hour and caused cramps in all the muscles that were not already cramped from scrubbing the floor. She decided to cook the lamb after all. It would last him an entire week unless he had company. Then she left another note on the pillow. "Forgive me . . ." she began plaintively. No; plaintive was out. She tore it up and wrote another. "Thank you for a lovely weekend." Breezy; so be it.

She left just before his last patient. She would be early for the group meeting, but that was all right. Suddenly she realized she hadn't eaten all day, even with all that food. Typical.

She told them all about her weekend.

"Jennifer Jones scrubbing the floor!" Sophy exclaimed. "I remember that! Barefoot, right? Kneeling, with her rear end up in the air, and then Gregory Peck slouches in behind her and kicks the door shut and . . ."

She nodded. "That's it," she said. "That's me." Then she finally allowed one of the sobs out; she had been secretly hoarding them. "I . . . feel," she sobbed, "I feel . . . so . . ."

"Well," said Tess wryly, "that's how it always feels when you play 'the girl.' "

"*Why*, though?" she wailed. "*Why* can't I have him and not lose myself?"

Tess shrugged. "Remember what Maria Ouspenskaya said to Vivien Leigh? Rapping her cane. 'You can have love or ze ballet. You cannot have bose.' "

"Bullshit!" said Laurie. "You can *too* have bose. Men have bose."

"They do not," said Tess. "They have ze ballet, or whatever their work is. But for love, all they have is this horrible game with someone who plays the girl."

She was still crying. "I'm going to London," she said. "He doesn't even care."

"Well, you're not *moving* to London," Wanda pointed out.

"I might as well."

"You get a nicer gay crowd there," Tess observed.

"Oh, Tess, I'm not ready for *them* yet. Maybe next life. *This* life all I want . . . just *one* time—"

"Yeah," said Sophy, "that's what we all want. Even Tess."

"Not Wanda," said Laurie. "Wanda's got 'The Good Part.'"

"So I've got other problems," Wanda retorted. "Like I can't talk to people. I've got the good part, and I've got rhythm, and I've got Stanley. Only I'm lonesome."

"We're all lonesome. Everyone in the world is lonesome," Margot sighed. "As my father said after his last divorce, 'Loneliness is a small price to pay for happiness.'"

"Besides," said Tess, "loneliness is healthy and natural. It's just had a bad press, like masturbation."

"I think maybe you shouldn't see Dr. Foxx for a while," Laurie said. "Are you writing?"

"*Writing?*" she cried. "I can't even *read*."

"Well, then, that's bad," said Margot. "Can you write when you're away from him?"

"Sort of. I write *to* him."

"So? That's better than cleaning his bathroom," said Sophy.

"Yes. I guess it is," she admitted.

"Could you go to London early?" Tess suggested. "Like for a vacation?"

"Sure, if I paid for it. *Penchants* is only paying for three days."

"So do it. Write to him from London."

"Write us too," said Laurie. "Keep carbons."

She hesitated, thinking. Why not? Would he be all right? Would he think she had betrayed him? Abandoned him? Lied to him? Like all his fathers and mothers? Like Murdock? She shook her head to erase the sudden memory of him in that awful room, the way she'd found him on Friday. *No.* If he insisted on self-destructing like that again, she wouldn't be there to clean it up. Or rather, she *would*— which was exactly why she'd better go to London. *Tomorrow.* She looked up at them, nodded, and took the wine Laurie had poured her. "Somebody else's turn," she said, and smiled.

LETTERS FROM LONDON
TO DR. FOXX, VERY CONFIDENTIAL
MY TURN
TOPIC: LOVE VS. NEED

The first time I was ever really aware of needing someone emotionally was when I was eleven years old. I had somehow got it into my head that Ronny Mosedale had to send me a valentine or I would die. I had not seen Ronny Mosedale since my ninth birthday party, when he came as a policeman and I was dressed as a little Dutch girl. He had moved out of Ann Arbor shortly afterwards, and I didn't even know where to. But I had found a picture that was taken at my ninth birthday party, and I cut out Ronny Mosedale's head and put it inside a gold locket, which I began to wear around my neck at all times, including in the bathtub, despite the fact that the chain, which was not real gold, left a distinct green line, so that my mother kept sending me back to wash my neck over. I wore the locket in order to ensure that Ronny Mosedale, wherever he was, would know to send me the valentine. Why, at the age of eleven, I would really and truly believe this was going to work, I can't tell you, but I really and truly did believe it. So much that on February 14, Valentine's Day, I was sick in bed with 101 fever. I have no idea what disease I had other than a burning need to be home when the mail came, so that I could open my valentine from Ronny Mosedale.

When the mail came and there was, mirabile dictu, no such valentine, I could not imagine what had happened except that poor Ronny had mailed it too late, and the mail was very slow wherever he lived, so it would probably not get to me until the 15th.

On the 15th I was well enough to go back to school; my fever had subsided, and the only remaining symptom was a heavy heart. Deep down I had begun to suspect that Ronny Mosedale had not in fact mailed it late. I came home that day, glanced at the mail, shrugged my shoulders and said something hateful about Ronny Mosedale. Then I went into the bathroom, tore his picture out of my locket, threw the pieces into the toilet and watched them go down, and I threw the locket in after them. Real gold.

I still have the picture of my ninth birthday party, me in the middle in my Dutch-girl dress, with my little white peaked cap on sideways, and next to me, this hole where Ronny Mosedale's head was. You can still see his body in the policeman's uniform.

I've hated Ronny Mosedale ever since that February 15th. Not because he didn't send the valentine; not even because he didn't love me. The only reason I hated him was that I had needed him so much. That's when I found out about need. It goes much better with hate than with love.

Would Dr. Foxx really fall apart if I didn't rush in to save him? Do I really want to know the answer to that? No.

TOPIC: MASOCHISM

I first got into masochism the night Warren Slavitt came up to me at a party and said I had terrific legs, and that if there really was a God, He would never have wasted them on me but given them to some good-looking broad like Ginny MacAdoo. This was why, Warren Slavitt said, he didn't believe in God.

It was not so much what he said as that in my innermost gut I agreed with him. Also, his saying it in front of twenty other people made me think that he was probably the sexiest bastard in Ann Arbor High School, if not the world. He was short and thin and not especially handsome, but he had a mean mouth and a vicious laugh, and that was obviously more than enough for me. Crying myself to sleep that night at the feet of the indifferent Frank Sinatras in my closet, I swore that I would love Warren Slavitt for the rest of my miserable life.

There are many other girls, including, I daresay,

Ginny MacAdoo, who would have raked their shapely unbitten pink nails across Warren's fresh face, or else said something devastating, like Hmph, and flounced off to throw themselves at someone more appreciative of them, with or without the terrific legs. I, however, knew instantly that I had found a higher calling.

In the months following his fateful remark, Warren Slavitt patiently showed me the masochistic ropes, so to speak. For instance, I learned never to cry in front of him. The Warrens of this world cannot stand to know that you are wounded—or rather, to have you bleed in public, thereby drawing attention away from them. When such a person has just announced to his entire class that he has brought this pig to the dance because what else would be lying around at the last minute when he decided he had nothing better to do, the point is not to make you cry; the point is to make everyone else gasp at what a mean sexy bastard he is to say a thing like that right in front of his date. It took me years to understand this. Without me, who would ever have heard of Warren Slavitt, the mean sexy bastard? Nobody. I made him. That's what I mean by a calling.

When I grew up—assuming that's what I did—I learned that there were two distinct types of masochist: the Orthodox, who go in for actual whipping and being shat on, and the Reform, who settle for the more subtle, emotional forms of same. My religion was always the Reform. I mean, when Warren Slavitt told me not to open my goddamn mouth in front of his friends or else, I did not ever have the slightest curiosity as to what the "or else" might involve; I got my jollies just from hearing him snarl it.

Of course I know that masochism is no longer considered a respectable career for a girl. Recently I heard a woman complain that her husband yelled at her for struggling out the kitchen door with a baby in one hand and a top-heavy laundry cart in the other. He couldn't stand seeing her all hot and sweaty and struggling like that. "Make two trips!" he bellowed. When she told the story, the woman said, "Isn't he impossible?" And she was beaming.

In any consciousness-raising group, that woman would be taken to task. Your husband is no longer allowed to treat you like that, and if he does, you certainly aren't allowed to go around beaming about it, right? So the question is, if masochism is out as a way of life; if it is no longer a worthy calling; if, in fact, it is nothing but a sickness—then what do I do with my years of training? I'm not really fitted for any other kind of relationship. I'm not even convinced there is another kind. Does Warren Slavitt have one? Who with?

I hope they are on the verge of discovering a live vaccine. A person like me could go in every week to a clinic and get a small dose of mean, sexy bastardism. By mouth, or any other orifice. And they would build up the strength gradually, so that after, say, twenty-five weeks, or years, you are immune. Then, when a Warren Slavitt says something devastating, or a husband bawls you out for struggling with his baby and his laundry while he stands there watching, or a Dr. Foxx gives you a dirty look for spilling his groceries, you'd have either a completely negative reaction, or no reaction at all. I keep thinking that if only they developed this vaccine, I might not get cured but at least I'd be rendered incapable of suffering to orgasm.

Lois Gould

Certainly I lie about it; I always have. Just as I have about my face. They're both to be concealed at all costs, or heavily doctored. Airbrushed out. Even the obituary photos should be airbrushed. "The late Soandso as she looked some years ago." How many years? Notice they don't tell you that.

Yesterday I got a reunion announcement from a school I attended for one year. One year, and they got me; I'm stamped on their permanent records. Notice that I'm not divulging which reunion it was, or even which school. I tore up the notice the instant it arrived and pretended I never saw it. Someone has made a terrible mistake, I said aloud, as if that rendered it undelivered. I am considering buying a red rubber stamp that says "Addressee Unknown," in case it ever happens again. I went to a lot of other schools, you know. Camps too. Come to think of it, I could get a stamp that says "Addressee Deceased."

I don't know what to do about my passport. You can fool around pretty safely with driver's license applications and job insurance forms. You can turn your ones into fours, or even sevens; you can turn your threes into eights. You can even fix up your old birth certificate if you're lucky enough to have one that's handwritten. But with the passports they seem to perforate the numbers, which is tantamount to searing them into the flesh. Even if I could duplicate the exact diameter of the little holes—and I've tried—I don't have the nerve. I know they would arrest me; some alarm would go off, bells and flashing red lights, and 15 burly government agents would seize that woman and take her away to wherever they take you when you tamper with government documents. It's

181

probably the same place they take you at the airport
when they find you have these curious metal objects
sewn into your undergarments. I figure the safest
possible course is not to plan on leaving the continental United States ever again.

I had an aunt who tried to lie about her age on an
application to renew her passport; it was something
of a scandal in the family. She got a form in the mail
from Washington D.C., which instructed her to state,
in quadruplicate, printing clearly, her exact reasons
for falsifying, or attempting to falsify, or withholding,
or attempting to withhold, vital information from the
United States government, on pain of smashing and
hitting. My poor aunt didn't know quite what to put
in the space provided. "I lied," is what she said, "because I have this friend in Mexico City whose passport says she is 12 years younger than I know her to
be, seeing as how we were in school together and she
was the class ahead of mine, and I thought if she can
have that age on her passport, why can't I?" She filled
this out in quadruplicate, of course.

Recently I read a newspaper article about a community in the southern part of the Soviet Union
where a person is never described as old. The word
does not exist in the language of this community.
They call those who get old "long-living people."
Which is nothing more than a rank euphemism,
though it has its points. But what they didn't say in
the article was at what age you have to admit that
you are a "long-living" person. I wonder if I could
get away with a few extra years in the southern part
of the Soviet Union. I wonder if they would ask to see
my passport.

I still remember telling my age in fractions—nine
and a quarter, ten and eleven-twelfths. I cared in-

*tensely about the exact hour and minute I was born,
so that even on my birthday I would be able to say
with impeccable accuracy that I was still 10 and
some fraction, right up to the stroke of 9:38 AM,
when I really turned eleven.*

*I guess I began lying just before my twelfth birth-
day. I did it (do they still?) in order to get into the
movies without an adult, in order to say "One adult,
please," to the cashier, and have her hand me a ticket
signifying that she believed me. I never suspected for
a minute that she didn't really believe me, that the
management was perfectly happy to let me pay twice
as much money as I needed to.*

*Later came lying to qualify for a summer job (per-
sons over 16), to get served a drink, and to get something in the mail ("Offer restricted to persons over
18.") I am over 18, I checked blithely in the appropriate box, when I was scarcely 16. Oh, please, I take
it back!*

*The first time I lied the other way, which is the
only way that really counts against you, was when I
was 24. I was applying for a job, and I had a folder
full of newspaper stories I had written, and in the
front page of the folder was my neatly typed resumé
which said "Age: 23." I had written the resumé when
I was 23, and I merely failed to update it. My 24th
birthday had occurred two full weeks before the job
interview, and I saw no reason to be picayune about
a thing like that. Besides, if we are being totally
honest, I wanted to be 23 a little longer.*

*"Is this correct?" the editor asked me, pointing
right at it. "Age: 23?" I expected to be swallowed up
at once into his four-inch-thick carpet. How did he
know? Was it the way my hair looked? My eyes?
The skin of my neck? Had I aged that much in two*

weeks? I was pretty upset. "Well, no, actually," I said, "I'm 24 now," trying to make it sound as if it had happened within the half-hour we had been chatting, so he wouldn't think that I was a liar, as well as old. "I have to change that. I turned 24 last Friday," I said, looking him right in the eye and defying him to pull out his dossier and tell me I had lied again, because he happened to have an irrefutable piece of paper that divulged my true date of birth.

After that, I lied all the time. Job applications, doctor's records; I no longer cared. When I went for a dental checkup I filched my dentist's charts that dated back to when I was three years old, because they had the year on them. My teeth may give me away—that's how they tell with horses, isn't it?—but they don't have it in black type any more. I brush very carefully now; I figure there's a good margin for error if you take excellent care of yourself.

I used to think about corpses being identified as Caucasian female approximately 36 years of age. How do they approximate that, exactly? Rippling skin on the inner thigh?

I find it gets increasingly harder to cover your tracks. People still ask, "What year did you graduate?" "Did you know Soanso? She went there; it must have been around your time." No, I don't know So-andso. That usually stops them, but not always.

Then you actually meet people who knew you in grade school, who were in your dancing-school class, who were your bunkmates in camp. What are they doing here? They've been assigned to your case by the Israeli secret police. They'll track you down to your hideout in Buenos Aires, where you've been living peacefully all these years as an unregenerate 18-year-old. Listen, please, I do not wish to renew *old acquaintanceships: go away. Or if you have to stand next to me, at least acknowledge that we have just this minute met. I swear to you, I've never seen that woman before in my life.*

These reunion things keep coming in the mail. Or to ask for money. It wouldn't be so bad if they didn't have these clever stamps all made up with my whole name, including the middle one that I dropped with a resounding thud the minute I found out I was allowed to. There it is, my middle name, along with the class number in bold black numerals, printed right out on the envelope so that even the mailman knows when I graduated, in case he wants to ad it to my zip code. Next year he'll drop a card in my slot saying "Season's Greetings, class of ——, from your regular postal delivery man." Addressee Unknown, do you hear? I'll fix him.

I suppose I shouldn't complain; I've been luckier than most people. Nearly every publication I've ever worked for on a regular basis is now defunct, thereby expunging most of my employment records. I no longer have the slightest idea what date of birth I put down anywhere.

I thank God I am not a royal person, whose birthday sets off a whole parade in front of the palace. I also count it among my blessings that I have never been a famous screen star, whose year of birth is published in The World Almanac, *and everyone automatically adds six, with a knowing smirk.*

Still, it would help if I had married frequently and moved abroad, discarding former names and official places of residence as I went, shedding them like snakeskins or used underwear. Hahaha, can't catch me! It also would have helped if I had dropped out of college and then gone back 10 or 15 years later to get my degree. Then I could say what year I graduated. No, I did not know Soandso; she must have been way before my time.

After a while you forget how far back it is okay to remember things. Fortunately they put all the old movies on TV, so I can always say I saw it there first. Obscure song lyrics are harder. How come I know every single word of "Der Fuehrer's Face," if I wasn't born until December, 1943? Well, my parents saved all these silly old records so that I grew up with it ringing in my ears. "Heil! Ffft! Heil! Ffft! Right in Der Fuehrer's face!" The trouble is, you have to think so much. How come you remember exactly what you were doing the day FDR died if you weren't even two years old? The best thing is not to participate in these discussions if you don't want to get into trouble. I'm learning to maintain a dignified silence most of the time—in deference to my elders.

It's like being a spy, though. I live in terror that someone clever is going to pounce one of these days. They will apply the thumbscrews to my nipples until I tell them what they want to know. Achtung! I lied. I was not born in December, 1943; I am easily 6 years older than I appear even in this light, thanks to remarkable plastic surgery. All right, six and a half years older. And I will turn into a long-living person before your eyes, and you have no idea how old and ugly you will think me.

P.S. I'm only fooling. I was so born in December, 1943. See, here it is right on my driver's license.

"Dear Peter Pan," he wrote. "Which of the following women never had the time or inclination to spend her birthday crying into a mirror?

Indira Ghandi
Margaret Mead
Marie Curie
Karen Horney
Simone de Beauvoir
Isak Dinesen
?

P.S. Whatever else a liberated woman is, I think that *first* she has to be a grownup. Foxx"

Chapter

TWELVE

THE EDITOR OF *Penchants* wondered if she'd be free for lunch the week she got back from London. Any day.

As editors go, Willard Hobbs, Jr., was notoriously sparing with lunches; in fact, he had never offered her one before. Coffee out of his executive filtered pot was about it, for largesse. Free-lance contributors generally got lunched by his managing underling, Frank Bickley, or by whichever senior editor would be butchering the writer's copy.

Willard Hobbs, Jr., was one of the half-dozen names that kept cropping up at the tops of various magazine mastheads. If you looked at these names carefully, you noticed how musical they were; all of them alliterated, had at least two sets of double letters in them, and sounded just as good backward as forward. Not just a first and last name, either; often there were three, with double letters in each one, or else a Jr. stuck rakishly at the end. No *Sr.*, mind you; they'd never put a Sr. at the top of a masthead. Sr. is definitely too old for the young readership market; the eighteen-to-thirty-fives wouldn't believe a word he edited.

You could picture the heads of the various canning corporations, which were financing magazines nowadays in order to diversify, sending out roving talent scouts across Middle America to pick up these fellows with magic names. In their mid-thirties now, clean-cut, conservative dressers, and don't forget the double letters. Nobody without double letters ever got to edit a major magazine. They'd get Donn Donnelly, who was over at *Home,* or Todd Barrett Gallagher, who'd just switched from *House* to *Garden World.* Or Willard Hobbs, Jr.

By the time he was thirty-seven, Willard Hobbs, Jr., had been editor in chief of four major publications, some of them twice, thanks to management shake-ups. She had done occasional pieces for him at *Targets,* at *Young American,* at *Family/Style,* and even at *Trip,* a promising little digest started by one of the smaller credit-card companies, which, despite Hobbs at the helm, folded after three exciting issues.

Hobbs had always liked her work. She was one of the few young free-lancers who handed in clean copy; Frank Bickley said he could practically slam it right into the magazine unread. Bickley had worked

with her closely at *Targets,* way back when; she was
on staff then, an assistant editor, before her marriage.
Bickley said she was one hell of a workhorse; did a
beautiful rewrite job on some of the worst hacks in
town and never complained. Bickley really appreciated that; as a rule, he couldn't stand women editors. The nicer their tits were, he said, the more often
they broke your balls on every paragraph they turned
out. They bled over their copy like it was *War and
Peace,* and anybody who expected them to meet a
deadline was the Beast of Buchenwald. Generally he
had to throw it back at them a dozen times before
he could run it; either that, or, if they were any good,
as she was, they got all hung up with their sex lives
and decamped to West Potato, N. J., before they'd
even learned to write a decent blurb that fit. Those
that stayed ended up pointing their tits at you, scream-
ing for bigger by-lines and refusing to get their little
hands dirty editing copy any more.

She had quit *Targets* when she got married, but
unlike most of them, she'd bounced back after a
couple of years. Divorced, and no kids. She had
turned out half a dozen pieces for them, and three
or four for other magazines. Nice pieces; solid; she
was still a worker. But that wasn't what they needed
her for at *Penchants.* They needed a workhorse on
staff. Somebody who could do heavy rewrite without
bitching, really slog through the shit-pile and turn it
into readable English. It would also help if such a
person had an occasional bright idea that wasn't
about Jackie Onassis' doctor's dog. But the main thing
was to bail Frank Bickley out. He was breaking his

ass to get the damn magazine out now; two of their
best men had quit within the past month, and Hobbs
himself was not about to get back in there and roll
up his sleeves. Hobbs had bigger corporate headaches
than *Penchants;* he was dealing with the money
people at ABZ, and if everything worked out, he
might be company president in a year or so. If it
didn't, he might be unemployed.

In short, this was definitely not the time to screw
up *Penchants'* newsstand sales, so he needed some
help for old Bickley. Somebody who could take Bickley's monumental guff, grind out clean copy, keep
his or her mouth shut and not be a pain in the ass.
Somebody they could afford; ABZ was hardly in the
mood to shell out for Harold Ross, even if they could
resurrect him. Somebody like . . . her. Hence the
invitation to lunch.

Bickley had suggested it. He'd heard she was
shacking up with some guy, but that he wasn't about
to marry her. Bickley had also heard that she wasn't
collecting alimony, so unless she was getting by on
her tits, she could probably use a nice steady job
with congenial types like Bickley and Hobbs. The
money might look goddamn good, in fact, to a broad
in that position.

"Better offer her a nice fancy title, though," Bickley had said, "because she'll have to give up her by-
line. I don't need Brenda Starr; I need somebody
to help me shovel the shit."

Hobbs had smiled. "But she'll get to look at
your big brown eyes every day, Frank."

"Yeah," said Bickley. "And yours. Like I said,

better offer her a nice fancy title. Assistant Czarina, or something."

"Leave it to me," said Hobbs. "Now get out of here and go sell some magazines."

"I never get to see you," Hobbs complained over his second Campari and soda. "Bickley keeps all the best-looking writers to himself."

She sipped her own drink. No comment; no smile, even.

"I liked your piece on Arnold Hatch," he said.

"Thank you. I liked it too."

"First-rate job," he went on, hailing the waiter with an elaborate finger-snap. "What did you think of him?"

"Couldn't you tell from the piece?" she asked, not unpleasantly.

"Got me there," he said, laughing.

They ordered the chicken Kiev. Everybody in that restaurant ordered chicken Kiev. Hobbs waved hello to Donn Donnelly, who was lunching with the author of next year's number one best-selling diet book. Hobbs squinted to see what they were eating. Raw clams. This year's number one diet book forbade raw clams. He sighed.

"Have you looked at the Futuro piece yet?" she asked.

"Hmm?" he said, frowning, trying to place it. "Futuro?"

"The fair," she said. "Vancouver."

"Oh, *sure*," he said a shade too heartily. "I just

saw it yesterday. *Great* piece. Really; reads just fine. How *was* the fair?"

"Couldn't you tell—" she said again, and this time they both laughed.

Halfway into the chicken Kiev was when he usually got to the point. "Ever think of going back to work?" he asked.

"I do work."

"I mean on staff. With your seat firmly glued to a posture chair instead of strapped to an airplane. Regular lunches"—he circled his plate with a forkful of chicken—"instead of dehydrated plastic steaks."

"I *like* flying around," she said. "It's fun."

"It's the little bottles I hate," he said. "And the tiny cardboard salt shakers. Everything is so goddamn precise."

"I *like* that," she said again.

"Well, *chacun*," he said, chewing, *"à son goût."* He glanced at his watch; this was taking somewhat longer than he'd planned.

He poured more wine and plunged in again. "Well, but have you ever thought of going back to editing? Bickley says you were damn good at it, way back at *Targets*."

She shrugged. "I could *do* it, but I didn't *like* it."

"Really?" he said. "I thought . . . Bickley said—"

"*Some* of it I liked. Thinking up ideas, working with *some* of the writers. But I *hated* editing copy, and I never had enough time to write my own stories; I was always having to rewrite somebody else's."

"Yes," he said. "Well. You never really moved up high enough, to where the *real* fun is."

"How high up is that?" she asked.

"You know, top level. Really planning the magazine, deciding what goes in it. *Molding* it."

She shook her head. "I guess it's not what I want. I guess I'd still rather write my own stuff."

"Trouble is," he said gently, "the woods are full of pretty good free-lance writers."

"Not all that good," she said. "I used to rewrite a lot of the big ones. Translated them from the original pidgin English."

He chuckled. "Yes, and their names are still the ones that sell magazines. Unfortunately."

"Whereas mine doesn't?" she asked. "Which explains why you never put it on the cover?"

"Let's just say," he smiled, "that it doesn't sell magazines *yet*. You're still very young, as writers go."

She smiled. "Not younger than many of those whose names one sees regularly on the cover of *Penchants*, however."

He ordered another bottle of Pouilly-Fuissé. "Let me give you an idea," he said in his authoritative sales-conference voice, "exactly how rough the newsstand competition is these days. Salesman walking to his bus, right? Passes a newsstand. Just enough time to buy a magazine. You've got forty-five seconds to sell him yours. Short of Tricia Nixon nude in the centerfold, you've got no hope except big names. There are eighty-five other magazines lying there reaching for his dollar."

"Okay," she said. "I understand that. But if you *build* a writer—a good, solid writer with good solid stories—why won't he buy that? I don't see."

He laughed indulgently. "What does your average magazine reader know about good solid writing? He knows if it sounds sexy, if it's a best-selling author, if it says he can drop ten pounds while he's sloshing his martini—*that's* what he knows. And women are the same. They'll buy a better orgasm, a better hamburger, and the terrible truth about face-lifts. If they were looking for good solid writing, they'd take that bus to the public library."

She shook her head, and he glanced at her sharply, wondering if she might burst into tears. "Look," he said gently, "let's say you're right, okay? Maybe you're right."

"Okay," she said, "I'm right."

He smiled. "Okay. Now, *assuming* you're right, that we need good solid stories by good solid writers, I've still got a problem. I have to get out a magazine. And I need you to help me."

"I *am* helping you," she said. "I'm writing good solid stories for you."

"That's not the help I need from you," he said. "I mean, yes, you're writing good stuff, great stuff, I love it. But that man at the bus stop, *he's* not responding; I mean, we're not getting his *attention*. Say you write *Crime and Punishment* tonight, and I excerpt it in the October issue, I *guarantee* you that that salesman won't buy it."

"Why not?"

"Beats the hell out of me," he said.

"Then I ought to quit writing for you."

"Exactly," he said. "And help me edit the magazine instead."

"Why *me?*"

"Because you happen to be a rare combination. You can do it all—writing *and* editing. And the fact is, a talented editor in this business is worth ten good writers."

"But I'd rather write."

He shrugged. "Write, then. As a friend, I can only tell you that you're wasting yourself. Come and learn how to be an editor; you could make it very big in this business. If you stick to free-lancing, you'll be just another good New York writer. A dime a dozen. It's up to you." He shrugged.

"If I did . . . if I were on staff, you mean I wouldn't get to write *at all?*"

He sighed. "I wish I could promise that, but I can't. I wouldn't want to lie to you. I need your brain working full time on ideas, and your hands working full time on copy, editing all those big writers who can't rub two sentences together and get a spark of decent prose going the way you can."

"All those big writers," she echoed, "whose names will be on the cover of *Penchants* instead of mine."

He smiled again. "Yours would be very big inside," he said. "On the masthead, along with mine."

By the time the second pot of espresso came, he was comparing the magazine business with the great Hollywood studios. "We make the stars; without us they'd all be busboys named Archie Leach."

She resisted a fleeting urge to point out what had become of the great studios.

Finally, twisting his lemon peel into her cup, he

got around to money. "Editors," he said, "make a hell of a lot more money than most writers."

"How much more?"

"You'd get everything that comes with the territory, I promise you that. Even a senior editor earns a lot more than you're making now. And we're talking about more than senior editor, aren't we?"

"How much would I get?" she asked again.

"Well," he said, draining his cup and signaling for the check, "suppose you think about whether you're interested in the whole idea. As we've discussed it. And then you call me—Monday?—and we'll talk about the details, okay?"

"Okay," she said. Numb. More than *senior* editor? *No* writing? A *lot* of money? Then she thought, They can't *stop* me from writing. After all, she'd be off nights and on weekends; she could still work on the novel. Joseph Conrad wrote nights. O'Hara . . . She could finish the novel and *then* quit, like Joseph Heller. Or she could grow up to be the editor of a magazine. *And* a novelist. Even Dr. Foxx would start clapping then. Deafening, thunderous applause. She could hear it. "When you wish upon a star . . ."

"I'll think about it," she said. "Thanks for the lunch, Will."

Before Hobbs had taken his hat off and lit his little cigar, Bickley was in his office. "How'd it go?" he asked.

Hobbs shook his head. "I don't know. I think she'd rather be Brenda Starr."

"She say no?" Bickley asked.

"She said she'd think about it."

"Mind if I take a crack at her?" Bickley said. "Between your boyish charm and my gruff good nature, the two of us ought to be able to hire one dumb broad to edit some copy."

"Go ahead," said Hobbs irritably, "but don't strain the budget."

"Who said anything about money?" Bickley said, swaying heavily on the balls of his small feet. He was the kind of heavy-set man who always looked as if he was about to topple over. "Brenda Starr doesn't grub for money," he said. "Brenda Starr is your dedicated career girl. Your indefatigable muckraker. She believes in her bosses."

"*Penchants Magazine,*" replied Hobbs, relighting his little cigar, "is not *The Daily Planet*. She starts raking muck around here, we lose eight of our major advertisers."

Bickley chortled. "Brenda Starr did not work for *The Daily Planet*," he said, tiptoeing out. "That was Lois Lane."

Hobbs called after him, "Just don't promise any of them anything I can't deliver. You hear me, Bickley?"

Bickley poked his large head back inside. "Who, me? Mrs. Bickley's baby boy Frankie?"

Hobbs waved him out. "Go sell some magazines."

Frank Bickley went Hobbs one better: dinner. Frank's wife, Sylvia, said it would be just the three of them, because they really wanted to see *her*. That was nice, she thought. Sylvia made a chicken

casserole, which Frank said was only 5.5 carbohy-
drate grams per serving, and then they had sugar-
free gelatin with sugar-free whipped cream, and
then Sylvia left them with the coffee and the coffee
liqueur and went to bed. It was nine-thirty. Neither
of the Bickleys bothered to say why Sylvia was
going to bed at nine-thirty, and she was much too
curious to ask.

So they sat in Bickley's living room whispering
in order not to disturb Sylvia, who was presumably
trying to sleep. She told Frank all about what Will
Hobbs had said at lunch, and he told her all about
how much fun it was at *Penchants*. He kept refilling
her little glass with coffee liqueur and a dollop of sugar-free whipped cream. She had worn a wide blue
suede cinch belt, encrusted with silver studs and
bordered with two feet of fringe, and the more
liqueur she drank, the tighter it felt. After a while
she couldn't stand it, so she stood up suddenly and
unsnapped it. "Whew," she whispered.

Frank Bickley peered at her from under his
heavy lids. "Lessee that insane thing," he said. When
she handed him the belt, he drew it slowly across his
knees and let it lie there, warming his lap. Then he
started running his fingers slowly over the silver studs,
left to right, and back again, as if he were reading
some kind of Braille pornography. Talking the whole
time about Willard Hobbs and all the fun at *Penchants*.

She sat down again, eying him uncomfortably.

"So," he said thickly, still caressing her belt, "you
think you want to be a big editor?"

"I don't know," she said, trying not to watch his hands and focusing carefully on the bookshelf directly above his head. It was full of books about preventing hair loss. "Editing has never been my secret ambition."

"My idea, you know," he said, pouring more liqueur. At six grams per glass, by his own count he had already used up two days' worth of carbohydrates. "Talked Will into it," he was saying. "I think we'd have a ball editing that magazine, you and I. Old Will, you know, old Will hasn't got his heart in it any more. Or his head, either. Old Will's getting to be a corporate structure all by himself. What old Will wants to be, when he grows up, is president."

"Of the country?" she said, thinking it was entirely possible.

"No, of the canning corporation." Bickley laughed, and then stopped abruptly, remembering Sylvia. "Yessir," he said.

"Not you, though, right?" she said.

"I," he said. And forgot what he was going to say. He sat for a minute, trying to remember.

"You just want to edit the best damn magazine you can," she prompted.

He nodded happily. "I am your original printer's-ink-in-the-vein, born and bred," he said. "Besides, I am not canning company presidential timber."

"Why not?"

"Too interesting," he said, "too fat and too Jewish."

"You're not Jewish."

"No, but to a canning corporation it's the same

thing. Too fat and interesting *equals* Jewish. Anyway, they don't promote from within; they just skim off the top." He gestured briskly at the cream on top of his liqueur, and knocked the glass over. As she reached for the glass, he reached for her. Somehow the belt stayed put across his knees, like a fringed lap robe. She edged neatly away. The hell with his liqueur glass, she figured; there wasn't much of a brown puddle on the white rug, anyway.

"So you and I . . ." he was saying, and then trailed off. "I mean you have . . . really nice tits." He reached out thoughtfully with his index finger, as if to show her just what he meant.

"Frank," she said calmly, "I guess I'll go home now and think about everything you've said." She stood up and held out her hand for the belt.

"Yes," he said, reaching again. "Really nice."

"Belt," she said.

"Stand still," he said, holding it up like a bull-fighter's cape. "I'll affix it on you."

"Well, I think—"

"Here you go," he said, flourishing it. She sighed indulgently and turned around. As he drew the heavy circle around her waist, he pulled her back toward him, so she grabbed his hands and pulled them together to snap the belt. He let go about half a second sooner than she expected, and both hands darted to her breasts. He squeezed. "Tits!" he cried. It was a cry of joy and reverence, like "Eureka!" or "Land ho!"

"I'll call you, Frank," she said, extricating herself. "Thank Sylvia; I hope she slept well."

That night she dreamed a revised version of her old editor fantasy. She was at a big editorial staff meeting, surrounded by Will Hobbs, Frank Bickley and about ten other men. "Just one more thing," Hobbs was saying. Frank Bickley grinned. "We'll excerpt those tits of yours in October. What do you think?"

All ten of the other editors turned toward her. "Me?" she said. "Why me?"

"Because you're a rare combination," said Will Hobbs, puffing hard on his little cigar, which was out. "Dime a dozen," one of the other editors murmured.

She hesitated, trying to decide. "I guess you're right. Okay."

Then Frank Bickley lunged over and shook hands. "Fun," he said, deftly unhooking her belt. "Only nine grams." He began nibbling the silver studs.

"But what about my name?" she reminded them. "On the cover."

"Oh, you'll definitely get everything that comes with the territory," Will Hobbs said, snapping his fingers. Frank Bickley winked again, picked up a large blue pencil and began to draw a thick line around each of her nipples. "By" he wrote on one; "line" on the other. "For an editor," he whispered happily, "she really has nice—"

His last word was drowned out by thunderous applause, but she knew what it was.

Chapter

THIRTEEN

WITHIN THE FIRST hour of the first day she reported for work at *Penchants*, she knew they'd conned her. Frank Bickley led her into a small dark room, a veritable *supply closet* of a room, at the end of the hall near his palatial estate. In the room were: one large desk; one secretarial posture chair; one typewriter; four piles of books strewn upon the floor. There was no lamp on the desk; all illumination came from the fluorescent bulbs flickering behind their opaque plastic ceiling panels like weak blue eyes in the sun. Apparently the books on the floor had belonged to a previous occupant of the room, who no doubt had been carted out during the night after suffocating.

Heaped upon the desk were several fat piles

of Xeroxed manuscripts, each neatly bound by two rubber bands, one horizontal, one vertical. "Hi!" said a memo atop one of the piles. "Pls read these soonest and let me know what you think. WH."

"Hi!" said another memo atop another pile. "Pls edit these; *heavy* editing. Urgent! Soonest! Love, FB."

"Hi!" she said, stifling a sob.

There had been no staff announcement made about her arrival—not an interoffice memo, not a note tacked to a bulletin board, not so much as a word to the central switchboard to connect her telephone extension.

Possibly you expected confetti in the lobby, she scolded herself sternly, and sat down to work. Once she'd had a job at a TV magazine called *Rerun,* setting up and editing an off-shoot monthly publication called *Channels,* with bright features about upcoming programs. She had worked there over a year, putting out *Channels* with a staff of two, and the switchboard operators never officially recognized either her existence or that of *Channels,* which had a paid circulation of 150,000. "Special project" was how her extension was identified on the official mimeographed directory that listed the telephone extensions of all personnel in the building. Everyone else was identified by name.

She shut the door and resolved not to cry. She had never cried in any office; it was a remarkable record for a heavy crier, and she was not about to spoil it now. She took a small sheet of clean paper out of the desk drawer and wrote down how much money she would be making, a figure which looked very impressive, especially in this room. Then she took all the pencils out of the drawer and began slashing away at the first manuscript in the "heavy editing" pile: "An Alcoholic Doctor's Foolproof, 80-Proof Diet."

She was on the last page when she heard Bickley's voice over her shoulder. "Hi, Manny." Bickley called everyone in the office Manny, except for Will Hobbs and the art director; it was his generic term of endearment for inferiors. "Uh," he said, swaying over her like a Bozo the Clown punching balloon, "you think we could get through that pile by tonight?"

"Sure," she said. "I've already got a call in for Rumpelstiltskin; he ought to be here any minute."

"Good girl," said Frank, grinning at her. He was just going down for a sandwich, he said.

"Eat hearty," she called after him.

Five minutes later Willard Hobbs stopped in. "Hi," he said jovially. "Got a minute?"

"Sure," she said. "I'm sorry I can't offer you a seat. Except this one."

"My God, isn't there a chair in here?" he exclaimed, rushing out into the hall, flailing. Somebody brought him a chair. "There, now," he said, as if he had just furnished their honeymoon suite. He had something important to discuss with her, he said as he closed her door. No one can hear me scream, she thought. Even if they weren't out to lunch, they would assume it came from the street. How would anyone know to look in this closet?

What he had to tell her was that she'd be pleased, he thought, to know that she was going to get a chance to do some writing after all: two short columns a month. One would be called "Show 'n' Tell," by Mel Curtis, the famous television comic, and the other would be called "Hobbs' Choice," by Willard Hobbs, Jr., the editor of *Penchants*.

She blinked.

Mel Curtis, Hobbs explained, had agreed to do ten columns a year for *Penchants* and they were very excited about signing him up. Three other magazines had been after him; Hobbs had had to wangle a hell of a lot of money out of ABZ to clinch it, but he and Bickley both felt that Curtis' name on the cover was a guarantee of fifty thousand extra newsstand sales a month, judging by the TV ratings of his new show.

Anyway, Curtis would drop by once a month to go over ideas for his column and give her a general picture of what he wanted to put in it. She'd be working with him on hammering it together.

"Ghosting it, in a word?" she asked.

"Working with him on it, yes," said Hobbs. "Now, this other thing," he went on smoothly, "is a new feature I just thought of, an editor's-note-to-the-reader kind of thing—you know, like a memo. What went on this month at *Penchants*. Readers like getting to know the people behind the magazine."

"Mmm."

"No big deal, this feature. I've already alerted everyone on the staff to feed you little scraps, newsy bits that might fit in. I imagine that with everyone shooting you stuff, you'll be able to wrap it up in half a day."

Lois Gould

"I imagine," she said, biting her lower lip to send a freshet of blood out onto his clean white shirt. The effort failed.

"Well, that's about all I had," said Hobbs, drawing himself up with a satisfied sigh. At the doorway he paused to survey the room. "Well," he said again, "you look as if you've been settled in here for ages!"

"Ages," she agreed, remembering to smile. If she'd had a forelock to tug, she would have saluted him.

Rumpelstiltskin never showed up; she assumed he had called in sick and the operator had been unable to locate her to deliver the message. Frank Bickley came back, though, two hours later and 7.2 grams heavier. Big sandwich. When she heard the patter of his tiny feet, she stuck her head out into the hall. "Frank?" she called. "Do you think I could have a lamp on my desk?"

"Gee, Manny," he said, "why didn't you speak up? Of course you can have a lamp. Good God, somebody, can't we get a lamp in this room?" he bellowed. Hobbs' secretary peered around the edge of her cubicle at the other end of the hall. "Mr. Bickley?" she called. "There's no one in the supply department now; it's lunchtime. I'll do what I can after lunch, all right?" It was three-ten P.M.

"There you are," said Bickley pleasantly. Possibly he thought the lamp had already been installed? She tried to look grateful. "Any time," said Bickley. "Anything else?" He glanced at his watch, indicating a busy executive doesn't have all day to stand around listening to petty complaints from his

209

Mannys. "Nothing that can't wait," she said cheerily, aiming her deadly basilisk eye at his departing head. Somehow he remained upright and disappeared whistling.

At six-thirty that night she finished the last of the "Urgent: heavy editing" manuscripts and left them on Frank Bickley's desk. He had gone out for a drink with a writer at five-thirty, making a special point of stopping in to tell her he'd be back at seven because he had to work all night.

Hobbs, of course, had never come back after lunch; he was attending a sales meeting with the ABZ board. Most of the staff left between five-thirty and six; presumably, nobody else had anything on their desks that Frank Bickley had to have tonight. Before leaving she forced herself to write a nice, light note to Will Hobbs. She had decided not to complain about anything until she'd finished the whole pile of manuscripts. Her desk was clean and she was taking home everything marked "Pls read and tell me what you think."

The note said: "Dear Will, Have we decided yet what my title will be? And when it will appear on the masthead? I'd like to notify my parents in Michigan—they're ordering engraved announcements. Love."

She also left a note on Bickley's desk, under the rubber band of "An Alcoholic Doctor's Foolproof, 80-Proof Diet."

"Dear Frank," said that one. "My lamp didn't come. Tomorrow? Love."

Then she took a cab to her group meeting.

Predictably, Margot prescribed massive doses of nose-punching, all around.

Laurie was annoyed with her. Nobody ever protested radically enough for Laurie. "Why the hell didn't you make a scene?" Laurie demanded. "Why the hell don't women ever make a scene? Men are *always* making scenes, yelling in the halls. Why can't *you* yell in the halls?"

"Because," she sighed, "women don't get away with yelling in the halls. They call you a hysterical bitch if you yell in the halls."

"Also," Sophy noted wryly, "they fire you. It's *their* halls."

"I bet nobody ever fired a woman for nose-punching," said Margot.

She shook her head. "Face it, Margot," she said. "In this world, some of us are nose-punchers and some aren't. Anyway, when did you last land one on anybody's nose at G. P. Putnam's Sons?"

Margot was not to be daunted. "Literally, maybe never. But at least I open my *mouth*. At least I call a bastard a bastard! At least I fight back!"

"I can't fight," she said. "I don't know how."

"You mean you don't think you'd win?" Sophy asked.

"I mean I don't think I *deserve* to win. Right now I could give you ten good reasons why I have no reason to complain. I'm well paid. All they're asking me to do is edit copy. I signed up for that; nobody twisted my arm."

"Nobody told you about the sweatshop working conditions either, did they?" shouted Wanda.

"What sweatshop?" she replied. "It's an air-conditioned office with free access to the water cooler."

"And no listing on the masthead," said Laurie.

"And ghostwriting for two other people," said Tess.

She sighed again. "There's no way to tell Will Hobbs that he's a bastard. Will Hobbs is the Barbie Doll of the magazine world. He makes Frank Bickley play bastard so he can play Mr. Clean. They're a classic team, like in crime movies. Hobbs is the one who says 'I'm on your side; I don't want my partner to get his big mean hands on you. If you don't play ball with me, I'll have to tell him, and then I'm afraid he'll kill you.' So you play ball with Hobbs, and then he sends Bickley in to kill you, anyway."

"I never go to those movies," said Wanda, yawning. "I think you ought to just go out in that hall tomorrow and start yelling."

"I think she ought to quit," said Tess.

"*Quit?*" she exclaimed, horrified. "I never quit any job in my life, except when I got married. I'm your original stickler and good sport. I do five times as much work as anybody, and never bitch. I stay till midnight if they ask me. I *volunteer* if they don't ask me. If anything goes wrong, I go home and cry so as not to bother them with my silly problems, and then I come back and work even harder so they'll feel sorry, and be nice, and let me go on playing with the big boys. Oh, please, let me stay on the team—that's how I got where I am."

"Yeah," said Laurie. "That's how, all right."

"Ever hear a man talk like you just did?" Sophy

asked. "Can you feature your friend Bickley talking like that?"

She tried to picture it, and giggled. "But I don't understand why they're *doing* it," she said. "They expect me to work my ass off, okay. I see that. I knew it before I took the job. They knew I was a greasy grind; that's why they hired me. But then, why wouldn't they be decent about the rest of it? What have they got to gain from making me miserable?"

"Maybe they figure," said Tess, "that the more miserable you are, the more you put out. That's how masochists operate—isn't that how you operate with Dr. Foxx?"

"I'm trying not to," she said.

"Couldn't you tell they'd pull something?" said Wanda. "I mean, you've worked with them; couldn't you tell they were bastards?"

"You know, she mused, "when I was just a free-lance writer, I used to go in there and if I had to use a typewriter they'd usher me into the biggest, poshest office. Anything I wanted—*they* sent out for *my* coffee. Any time I dropped in, everybody was all smiles. Big hellos; big 'Look who's here!' So now look who's here. You'd never know it was the same person."

"They *own* you now," said Laurie. "When you own the woman, you get to do anything you want to her. It's called conjugal rights."

"That's ridiculous," said Tess. "She's free to quit."

"Is she?" asked Margot. "What if she wants to go back to free-lancing? How many assignments would Frank Bickley give her?"

"You're right," she said, thoughtfully. "And Hobbs

would let it drop here and there that I'd flipped out, or screwed up somehow, or was all of a sudden just a pain in the ass. All of a sudden." She paused, remembering Hobbs' voice: "Writers are a dime a dozen in New York . . . Your name doesn't sell magazines."

"You're right," she said again, and burst into tears. Just like a woman. Tears of rage: the ultimate toy weapon.

"Know what I think?" mused Sophy. "I think Hobbs has no intention of putting her on the masthead."

"Oh, come on," said Margot.

"No, I mean it. Why should he? He's paying her well. Like she said, she can't just walk out in a huff, so he can keep stalling as long as he wants. Next month, he can say. And then, he's sorry, but they just couldn't catch the title page in time—some problem with the printer. He could hide her there for a year without telling a soul!"

"But why would he do that?" said Margot.

"Because," said Sophy, slowly sipping her wine, "the minute he puts her name up on that masthead, he's got two problems he doesn't have now. One: the rest of his staff—the *boys*—get mad. Lots of interoffice grumbling. Who the hell is she? Is Hobbs balling her? How come she gets this big title ahead of us? Morale problems! He's got to soothe all those ruffled peacock feathers, right? The longer he can put that off, the better. He's very busy, Willard Hobbs; he's sniffing around for a big promotion or something, right? So if he keeps her hidden for a while, if it's just a shameful little secret between him and Bickley, nobody gets upset."

"What's the second problem?" asked Margot.

"Ah," said Sophy, "that's the *real* clincher. The second problem is that if he puts your name up on the masthead, he's making a public announcement that you're valuable. Everybody else in the business knows who you are, and that you're there because Hobbs needs you. You've got this big job, so you must be good. Maybe somebody even gets the bright idea of hiring you *away* from *Penchants*. More money *and* a desk lamp! They do that all the time, right?"

She nodded, mesmerized.

"It's a well-known fact that your Willard Hobbs types don't go around putting little girls way up on their mastheads just because they have nice tits."

"Funny you should mention that," she murmured with a wry smile.

"Anyway," Sophy went on, "as I see it, he's building up this atomic stockpile. You're his secret weapon! You'll work your little ass off and keep your little mouth shut, he'll get the magazine out better and faster and neater, eventually he'll get his promotion, and then everybody's happy! It's beautiful! I think Willard Hobbs is one very smart Barbie Doll!"

"Well, I think it sounds crazy," said Margot. "They don't do that."

"Yes, they do," she said slowly. "It happened to me once, just like that. Over at *Currents*. I stuck it out there for a whole year without a by-line or a listing in the phone directory. All I got was well paid. Nobody in the world knew who was putting out that little digest."

"See!" exclaimed Sophy. "Does Hobbs know about that?"

"Sure he knows," she said.

"Well, then!" Sophy spread her hands eloquently. "The prosecution rests."

"Ghost writers," Laurie said. "It's true! Ghost writers are never revealed to the public. The minute their names get visible, they quit being ghosts."

"Better learn to fight," Wanda said. "If you keep quiet, they'll bleed you to death, and nobody will ever know but us."

"Yeah," said Margot. "If you can't punch them, at least yell."

"Try yelling rape," said Laurie. "Because that's what it is."

The following day her desk was piled high again. There were no memos saying "Hi," however; notably no memo from Hobbs about how and when, if ever, she might expect to make her formal debut as a member of the staff of *Penchants*. There was also no desk lamp.

She shut the door of her office and set to work. Suddenly the telephone rang. She jumped, just as she had at Dr. Foxx's house. How could it be for her? But it was; it was Dr. Foxx.

"I found you," he said playfully.

"Yes," she said. "I'm here." And for some reason just saying that made her cry—in the office, right into the telephone extension that had somehow

216

been hooked up. It was, in fact, hooked up to Bickley's office, so that Bickley's secretary would pick up all her calls and announce "Mr. Bickley's wire." This was how the switchboard had been instructed to handle her calls.

"Hey," he said. "What did I say? What is it?"

"Not you," she stammered. "Me." He *would* have to sound tender; that always set her off.

"Hey, come on," he said gently, "no tears in the office."

"I know," she sobbed, "but I don't know where else to put them right now."

"I'll take them," he said. "What time do you finish tonight?"

"Six, supposedly."

"Want me to pick you up at six, supposedly?"

She nodded, sniffling.

"Well?"

"I mean yes," she said, still sniffling.

"Downstairs," he said. "I'll be in the car."

"Make it six-oh-five, then," she said.

"Okay, six-oh-five, but no later. I can't double-park there; it's a one-way street."

"Six-oh-five," she said. "I promise."

The day elapsed. Mel Curtis, the famous TV comic, came in to chat with Hobbs and Bickley about his cover-line billing, his picture and the size of his by-line. She was invited in to meet him. He had no ideas for his column, but promised he'd come up with something. "Don't worry," said Bickley, "we'll let Manny here do the worrying—right, Manny?"

As for "Hobbs' Choice," the frothy mix of staff

anecdotes she was supposed to whip up around Hobbs' picture and facsimile signature above it, the art director had asked if she could possibly have it done by the following day. "Plenty of time for that," Bickley assured her. "Tomorrow." Only nobody had given her a single item. She would have to stop in at every department and plead for amusing scraps. Maybe that was the fun Bickley had talked about so much.

At ten minutes to six, Bickley stuck his head in her door and said that all Mannys were wanted in Hobbs' office for a short meeting.

"But I have to leave at six."

"What?" he snapped. "This is *important*." His bushy brows knitted like a feathery thundercloud, and he lumbered off.

"Okay," she said. She scrambled to put things together for a lightning exit and raced down the hall to Hobbs' office.

He wanted to ask her whether she liked red with a white logo, or blue with an orange logo, for the October cover. "Red with white," she said.

"Did you know," said Hobbs, leaning back in his swivel chair and blowing cigar rings, "that people in supermarkets tend to buy more orange-and-blue boxes than any other color combination?"

"No," she said, "I honestly didn't," sneaking a surreptitious look at her watch.

Bickley caught her and frowned.

"It's a fact," said Hobbs gaily, "I just got this report from a motivation research outfit. Blue with orange, and orange with blue. Yellow is also big; how do you like the yellow with a black logo?"

She looked at the yellow with the black logo. "Somehow," she said, "it makes me think of a bumblebee. I'm allergic to bee stings," she added, "so maybe I'm no judge."

It was Hobbs' turn to frown. "What about the blue with the orange then?" he said.

"It's nice," she said, "but I still like the red one." It was six o'clock. "I'm sorry," she said rising slowly from her seat as if she were being pulled against her will by invisible wires. "I have to go now," she murmured, hearing her voice disappear. "I have . . . a doctor's appointment."

Hobbs' mouth opened in a perfect small ring behind the one he had just blown, then clamped shut around the plastic mouthpiece of his cigar. He drew on it heavily.

She stumbled out, feeling their eyes burning four neat small holes in her back, each approximately the size of the flowing ash on Hobb's cigar. One, she imagined, was blue with a yellow center, and one red . . . Bathed in a fine mist of icy sweat, she raced back to her cell, picked up all the "Pls read and tell me what you think" manuscripts and tore down the hall to the elevator.

"What's that?" said Dr. Foxx, eying the Xerox paper mountain in her arms.

"Stuff I have to read," she said, settling carefully into the front seat after removing two cans of tennis balls and his mail.

"No, you don't," he said. "You get off at six, supposedly, didn't you say?"

"Yes," she said, "but—"

"Then I'll take care of those for you till tomorrow." He reached over and lifted the pile off her lap.

"But—"

"You can have them back first thing in the morning," he said, shoving them under his seat with his bank statement and the notes for a lecture he was giving tomorrow on "Life Styles of Obsessive-Compulsives."

"I can't read that stuff in the office," she said.

"Why not?"

"Because that's when I have to write two columns and edit a major piece called 'Making Impotence Work *for* You.'"

"Then you can read it the next day," he said. He looked over at her just in time to catch the first tear glinting in the light of a passing streetlamp. When he abruptly stopped the car, right in the middle of Third Avenue, she gasped, and then saw it was for a red light. Usually he paid no attention to red lights on one-way avenues, except to race through the next six intersections until he caught up with the green part of the cycle again.

"What *is* it?" he demanded.

"Nothing," she said, and then told him. All of it.

"Bastards," he kept muttering. "Bastards."

"I know," she said finally, "but I can't do anything about it."

"Yes, you can," he said firmly. "Nobody has to take that crap."

"But look at all the *money* they're paying me to take it," she wailed. "That's how *they* look at it. She's getting paid, so what's her gripe?"

"Her gripe," he replied, "is that she's entitled to decent working conditions and full credit for the work she does—just like *they* get."

"*Entitled,*" she said. "That's funny!"

"I thought so," he said dryly. "Did Hobbs ever suggest any specific title?" he asked a few minutes later.

"Yes, one," she said. "Before I took the job he suggested maybe 'Assistant to the Editor.' I said no."

"Good for you," Foxx said. "Sounds like an executive secretary. Any time I see that title I assume it's the person the boss sends out with a check to buy his wife's Christmas present, someone he trusts to pick out just the right thing."

She nodded. "But they've already got an assistant managing editor, and an articles editor, and even a special-features editor. So what's left? He's got to invent something."

"What about managing editor?"

"That's Bickley's title."

"I know, but why can't they have *two?* Co-managing editors. I've seen that on lots of mast-heads."

"Bickley would have apoplexy," she said.

"So he'll switch to a low-fat diet," he said. "Anyway, that's what Hobbs promised you: the three of you up there together, like the Supremes. All that fun editing the magazine together. So what could be more together than co-managing editors? That's how I see it."

She leaned over and kissed him on the cheek.

"So it's settled, right?" he said, eying her anxiously.

"Right," she said, and smiled.

He parked the car outside his house and locked it, so that the manuscripts would be absolutely safe till morning. Not that anybody would ever bother breaking into his car.

The next day when Bickley hove into her office, thrashing his arms and yelling, "Where the hell is—" she replied calmly, "I'm reading it."

"Oh," he said. "Well, then where the hell is—"

"I'll get to it this afternoon," she said. "After I finish this."

He turned somewhat red, with a white logo, and lumbered back to his office.

At twelve-thirty she went out to lunch, just like all the other kids, and at three-fifteen she marched into Hobbs' office, smiling pleasantly, and announced that she'd decided how she wanted to be listed on the masthead. "Co-managing editor," she said. "Okay?"

Hobbs opened his mouth into one of his little silent O's, and then snapped it together before anything could escape. A little later she saw Bickley enter Hobbs' office and close the door, and about twenty minutes after that, Bickley dropped in to see her. He was more of a purple now, with maybe a green logo, and a smile that needed heavy editing.

"So," he said, "we're co-managing editors. Isn't that ducky? You stupid bitch."

She bit her lip. "Frank," she said evenly, "do you think you could ask your secretary—when she picks up my phone, I mean—if we're co-managing editors, to say my name instead of 'Mr. Bickley's wire'?"

He did an imitation low bow from his forty-one waist, turned on his heel and wheeled out, slamming her door. She sighed. They weren't going to have any fun, after all.

The masthead of *Penchants* listed her name (under Frank Bickley's), with the title Managing Editor, exactly once, five months after she had joined the staff. She appeared in the October issue. A banner month, October. They had gone with the blue cover/orange logo. They had a glossy black coverline hailing the hilarious magazine debut of TV's funniest man, Mel Curtis. Inside they had *Penchants'* own Willard Hobbs, Jr., wearing his Barbie smile, blowing a perfect cigar ring above "Hobbs' Choice," a bright, breezy fifteen-hundred-word collage of friendly gossip about all the folks and their doings backstage at *Penchants.* Well, not quite all the folks and their doings.

Still further inside was the last piece she ever wrote for *Penchants* under her own by-line. It was her London assignment, a free-wheeling interview with the newest darlings of the rock subculture, three

ten-year-old girls who sang filthy radical feminist
lyrics but wore white confirmation dresses and black
patent-leather party shoes, thereby alienating everybody. Not a bad piece, Bickley had said, chortling
over every pungent line. They had cut it in half
and run it in the back of the book, in between the
mail-order truss ads.

She took her week's vacation over Labor Day,
and spent it at Laconic Beach with Dr. Foxx. Bickley's secretary thoughtfully sent her an advance office
copy of the October issue, and Bickley thoughtfully
clipped a note on it, saying, "Congratulations."

She riffled quickly through it and then handed
it wordlessly to Dr. Foxx. "Bastards" was all he said.

"I can't go back there," she murmured.

"Yes, you can," he replied, holding her. "But
you don't *have* to."

"No," she whispered, fighting the tears. "I *have*
to, but I *can't.*"

"Ssh," he said.

Though she was in and out of tears most of the
week, somehow he remained tender and tolerant.
"How come," she would sob at him, "you're so tender
and tolerant all of a sudden? You hate it when I cry."

"No," he said. "I only hate it when you cry over
me."

"Oh." And she would resume crying into the
pillow, or against his chest, or into the salad, or
the Racquet Club pool, or the shower.

"What would you do," he asked, "if you didn't
have to go back?"

"Write," she said. "Finish my book." She hadn't

224

touched the book since she'd begun working at *Penchants*. "But it's impossible. I haven't got a contract. I don't even have enough pages to show anyone to *ask* for a contract. And if I quit *Penchants* like this, I'm through as a magazine writer."

"Well," he said, "I doubt that. I can't see Will Hobbs taking the time to rush around ruining your good name. It wouldn't be that important to him."

"He wouldn't have to rush around. He'd just drop it into the chicken Kiev at Le Weekend; it would be served to fifteen editors simultaneously."

He shook his head. "I can't believe he'd care enough. I'm sure you could still get good assignments. The *Journal, McCall's*—they all know you. You're still a pro, after all, the workhorse with the clean copy, remember?"

Her eyes were filling again. "Dime a dozen," she said. "I don't want to hustle any more. I don't want to write about the Arnold Hatches of this world, or the rock star kiddies, or the world's fairs. I want—"

"I know," he nodded. "To be a *real* writer."

"Yes," she said miserably. "And I can't."

He shook his head again, but stopped arguing.

Later that night, in bed, he mumbled, "What if . . ." and then, "No. Crazy idea."

"What?"

"Nothing," he said. "Ssh." And he turned toward her, and she turned toward the wall so that all the curves and hollows fit. But neither of them slept well.

"What if . . ." he started again at breakfast. "No."

"Why not?" she said this time, laughing.

"Because it's an old crock, this house," he said,

"and nobody in their right mind would try spending a winter out here all by themselves writing a book."

Her eyes opened wide, and then narrowed again quickly, like Venetian blinds behind which someone is watching secretly.

"Of course, there's the space heater," he was saying to himself. "And the fireplace in the bedroom . . . No." All of this in an anxious half-mumble, as if he were expecting someone to arrive at any minute and wanted to work out what he was going to say before they came.

"Goes down to ten below zero," he muttered. "Sometimes the bay freezes solid enough to skate on."

Her stomach was churning exactly the way it had when her seventh birthday was coming and she'd overheard her parents talking about this practice board that once belonged to Eleanor Powell. She didn't tell him that, though; she tried to act as if she weren't really there, in case he talked himself out of it. She held her breath, waiting.

"And no phone," he went on. "I always shut it off October one. She'd be completely isolated here. No car . . . it's crazy."

"No, it's *not!*" she blurted at last. "I'd be fine, I have my bike, oh, please, it's—" and finally hurtled into his arms, because if she could only hug him hard enough, it would come true; would render him incapable of not giving her that sacred old practice board.

"The windows aren't even airtight," he exclaimed, struggling to unwind her deathlike grip. "Look!" He went over and rattled an ancient pane in its splintering wood mullion. The house was a genuine antique, one of those humble frame cottages you see along the older roads in eastern Long Island; early settlers used to house their shepherds in such houses and old photographs of them hang in the local libraries. Their doors were all put in lopsided, and their floors are so warped that you feel as if you are walking on a listing ship in troubled waters. They are built flat on the ground, like hotels slapped on a Monopoly board, and nobody understands why they are standing at all, after more than two hundred years.

"You'll get pneumonia in this house," he said. "I'll come back in April to find your stiff blue body in my historic sleigh bed, and I'll have to explain to your parents that I warned you."

"I promise," she said gravely. "I *promise* I won't die."

He laughed, then frowned again. "No," he said, "I forgot. I don't think you could afford the rent."

"*Rent?*" She studied his face for signs of kidding. "How . . . how much would you want?"

"Well," he said, thinking hard. "I rented it once for the summer, for two thousand dollars. But of course—"

"Two thousand dollars? But nobody would rent it in the *winter*. Without *heat?*"

"That's true," he said. "Tell you what. I'll let you have it for—" He broke into a big mischievous grin, which she caught.

"You *rat!*" she cried. "I was about to offer you every cent in my checking account. Plus I'd clean the house up for you. I'd fix things, insulate the windows. I'd even . . . I was even going to say I'd finish papering the kitchen!"

"I'll take it," he said. "Not the money. But the papering job. It will give you something to do if you get blocked."

"Rat!" she said again. "I love you."

"Don't die on me, though," he said. "You promised."

Mr. Willard Hobbs, Jr.
Editor
Penchants Magazine

Dear Will:
This letter is for both you and Frank. An emergency has come up in my personal life, which makes it impossible for me to return to work as scheduled. I'm sorry to have to let the team down like this; I hope you both know me well enough to understand that I'd *never* do it if there were any other choice.

Working with you these past months has meant a great deal to me. I hope I've justified your faith by doing the kind of job you wanted. I've done my best.

As soon as I can possibly return to magazine work, I hope you'll ask me back to write again for *Penchants*, on a free-lance basis. I hope you'll want me back on the team.

In the meantime, I'll miss you both.

She signed it "With much affection and professional esteem."

"That's disgusting," said Dr. Foxx angrily. "Let-

ting them think you've gone crazy, or gotten knocked
up! I thought you'd be strong enough to tell the
truth. That they lied to you, and cheated you, and
that you don't have to play games with guys who
cheat. If you walk off the court mad, in the middle
of a game, you let them know *why*. Otherwise you're
a spoiled brat, or a coward, or both."

"But I can't walk off their court like that!" she
cried. "If I ever want to play again, it's the only court
in town. Don't you understand?"

He said that *he* understood, all right, but that
she didn't. He said that someday she'd have to grow
up and quit pretending she was still this nice child
who never made trouble, never hit back or even
yelled *ouch* when someone hit her. Who just curtsied
and said, "Thank you, I had a lovely time," and then
went home to cry. Someday, he said, she'd face the
fact that the Bickleys and the Hobbses had never
loved her, and never would, no matter how nice
she was, and that was when, he said, she would be
a *mensch*—or, rather, a woman.

Before she mailed the letter she called two members of her women's group and read it to them on
the phone.

Margot agreed with Dr. Foxx. "Tell the bastards
the truth!" she said. "They *screwed* you!"

"What if I have to work with them again?" she
said. "What if I never get to be a big famous writer?
Why should I go around burning my bridges if I
have to get back across the river in six months?"

Laurie didn't think she should quit at all. "Women
always run away," she said. "That's why women never

get to run anything else. They can't stand the heat, so they get *back* in the kitchen."

"That's not where I'm going," she said.

"Aren't you?" said Laurie. "Aren't you going into hiding in Dr. Foxx's house?"

"I don't think so, Laurie," she said slowly. "I don't think I'm hiding at all. I think I'm coming out."

Laurie wished her luck, anyhow, and later Sophy called to do the same; Margot had told everyone that she wasn't coming back to the group. Sophy said she thought that what she was doing was great—very brave—and that *Penchants* had been a fat waste of time, and that the group would miss her, but that she should write well and not worry, and they all loved her.

"Thank you," she said, crying into Dr. Foxx's telephone that was being disconnected on October 1.

At eleven o'clock on Sunday night of the last weekend in September, she stood in the dirt road outside the sagging door of Dr. Foxx's crazy old house and waved goodbye to his battered car. The last thing he said, leaving, was to forget about the wallpaper; he'd decided he didn't like the little frying pans either. "Just write well," he said, "and don't die."

He had confiscated her entire supply of Dexamyl. "You don't need these," he said. "Dumbo didn't need his magic feather. He could fly all by himself, and he was only a dumb little elephant with floppy ears, remember? Whereas you"—and he stopped talking just to look at her a long quiet time—"whereas you," he concluded softly, "are terrific."

"I love you," she called now, letting the noise of his motor swallow it. He stuck an arm out to wave back. She could barely see his head through the mountains of clothes and papers he had piled in the back seat. He always took home all his summer shirts, in case October turned out unseasonably warm. He also took all his tennis shorts, racquets, sneakers and a dozen cans of balls in case he wanted to play in town over the winter. Which he somehow never had, but maybe this year. Also, he took home all the magazines he had brought out in July, to clear them out of his apartment and get through them out here when he had more time. Somehow he never seemed to get through them out here either, so he had to cart them all back to the city. Maybe he'd have more time in the fall.

Especially this fall, he had said, indicating that he would miss her but not saying it. "I'll miss you," *she* said finally. "Write about that," he replied.

She walked back to the house, feeling the wind, already chilly, through her shirt. Leaves were blowing and the two small rhododendron bushes he had planted looked doubtful. She shivered slightly. On the little rag rug inside the front door lay one of his tennis socks; he must have dropped it staggering out with the last bundle. She picked it up and stood there for a minute, holding it.

Chapter

FOURTEEN

SHE SPENT THE first week of October on her knees, attacking the historic dirt in Dr. Foxx's house. She sponged up lakes of gray water and then cried into them, gazing at her sudsy reflection. The gray never lifted; the suds vanished; the water never ran clear. She scoured the tub and the toilet. Rust stains remained, streaming down their sides like failures that cannot be erased from your high school record. She collected the loose nails in his utility room and sorted them into glass jars. She swept the peeling paint off the window sills, straightened the misshapen wire hangers in his closet and pasted small vinyl flowers over the cracks in the bedroom walls. Wall flowers. She biked into town to stock up on hard cheese, sugar-free cola, more sponges.

Nothing helped. The house was controlled by its dirt, and she was an intruder. She wrote nothing. She never entered the living room, where her typewriter sat sulking on an old school bench. In the living room she could still feel the grit under her bare feet, could see the cobwebs spanning musty corners, softening their sharp lines into pale blurry clouds. Under the pots of dried flowers she had put on the tables, there were small clean circles showing how much dust lay everywhere else. O, the circles cried, look at the dust around here.

She tried to work in the bedroom, with a notebook and pens, but her eyes would travel the cracks that now disappeared under the little flowers, like delicate stems. She fell asleep often, waking with starts of guilt to find that three hours had gone. Or six. Or the day.

TO DR. FOXX: UTTERLY CONFIDENTIAL

MY TURN

TOPIC: SELF-CONFIDENCE

I am still on page 27. I have rewritten pages 1–26 approximately ninety-four times. No one in the world is waiting for this dumb book. Whatever made me think I'd be a writer when I grew up? I am not a writer; I am not grown up; I am wasting my life and your house.

She biked to the post office in town twice a week and checked his mailbox. He wrote to her, care/of himself. It was the first time he had ever sent her letters. "I'm waiting for the book," he wrote. "Get to work or I'll have you evicted as an undesirable tenant." He signed it "Love, Foxx," which made her cry. "Love, Foxx." Love? Foxx?

By the time she had truly accepted the terms of her stay in this house of his—that he had left her alone here to fend not for him but for herself; by the time she had stopped rearranging the old pictures—Admiral Byrd at the Pole and the sepia etching of Mark Twain—over the major cracks in the living room; the print of Whistler's mother above the old sink in the rear utility room; the sampler of the Lord's Prayer over the bed—by the time she had managed to stay awake eighteen hours of a day without cleaning, without even *thinking* of cleaning; by the time she had actually begun to write—not to rewrite, but to *write* —it was mid-November.

TO DR FOXX: UTTERLY CONFIDENTIAL

MY TURN

TOPIC: ALONE VS. LONELY

I am learning that alone is different from lonely. Not always, but at its best, very different. Alone can actually be nicer than together, if you know how. Remember the song "Me and My Shadow"?: "At 12 o'clock, we climb the stair; we never knock, 'cause there's nobody there"? Nonsense; I'm there. And aren't I terrific to be with? Look, for instance, at the way my body moves in the mirror. Smile encouragement. Have I ever smiled at myself in a mirror before?

No. I've only scowled, or flinched, or noticed what
had to be fixed immediately, because look at it, it's
awful. After a long time alone, I'm learning to smile
at myself. I'm beginning to appreciate this person; I
even like playing with her. We play solitaire. That's
another beautiful English word: solitaire.

The sun is gleaming on the ice now, as on a big
white metal shield. The last ripples of moving water
froze where they crested, like children playing statues.
In the village they say the bay has rarely frozen this
solid before—miles of imprisoned water. Utter still-
ness. I stare at the single strip of houses, safely far
away and empty, strung along the beach directly
across the bay. Small whimsical shapes a child would
draw across a long ribbon of shiny paper. Flat triangles and low boxes, a cube, a pyramid. Origami.
Directly in front of the window I can see a clump of
tall beach grasses, sparse and angular, bowing their
long heads to the wind like respectful mourners heaving appropriate sighs. Ah, yes, she was a good woman,
a good soul. Shards of wood, thin stumps really,
stand behind them, rude and upright like remnants
of the future, defying scientists to decipher them.
Who was I that I alone stood erect all this time? Who
was I to survive?

Behind the grasses and the wooden relics, a single
bright block of crumpled ice catches the sun. There
are other patches too, great dark ones, glistening like
stains, water that has come unfrozen, dark reservoirs
of blood rushing under the smooth skin. It's shameful
to see how beautiful wetness can be, exposed like
wounds or secrets.

Whenever the wind stops, the grasses stand
straight for an instant, and then turn toward the
glistening wet spots, as if they might have made

*some sound. There is another stirring, another rustling.
Yes, a good soul. Either she was happy here—certainly she must have been happy sometimes—or else
she will be at peace now; in either case, it is hardly
our responsibility.*

*I can work at this window for hours at a time,
writing in longhand on lined paper, and either I am
happy here or else I am at peace, now. I am alone.
I have never felt less lonely.*

Hey, you know what? I'm functioning!

Dirt still surrounded her; hard winter dirt now,
crusted, pungent with dampness, not the soft dry
summer soil that sighed in corners and moved on.
But it no longer mocked her; it contained no silent
accusation. She was at last only a guest in this house,
minding her own business of writing in a less than
spotless spot—and what of it? They had arrived at
an understanding, she and this ancient place of his.
They disliked each other and had fought to a bitter truce; now they would exchange cool nods in the
corridors. They would give each other room to be
themselves. The house would fill itself with dirt; she
would fill herself with her own words spilled on
paper.

When the serious cold came, she learned to deal
with it by playing hide and seek. He had taught her
how to flee from room to room, shutting different
combinations of doors to trap the heat in small spaces.
She huddled near the fireplace, close enough to make
her eyes water and color her cheeks; never close
enough to stop the tingling in her toes. She wrapped
herself in his old sweaters and the blankets that

smelled of mothballs and the attic cedar chests in which she found them. She wore two pairs of the old tennis socks he had left, and a pair of his big knitted gloves that had moth holes in spite of the cedar chests and camphor balls. Though her own leather gloves, lined in rabbit, were warmer, she could not move her fingers in them to write. And the need to write was constant now.

She began to wake in the mornings at seven, she who could never get up before ten, who had always been half asleep at her office desk, whipping herself into productivity. At seven, numb with cold, trembling with excitement, she would wake and start the fire again, lighting the old coal stove in the kitchen and pouring more kerosene into the space heater. She ate standing up, pacing, thinking, or else huddled before the fire. She woke with impatience, phrases stirring in her head. She woke smiling.

There was no more drowsiness over the notebook; the old midday torpor had lifted like grayness after rain. Even at night words raced each other in her sleep, prodding her. She would stir, thinking, Write it down! I should write it down now; I'll forget it tomorrow. And sometimes she obeyed; shaking off blankets and sleep at three or four A.M., lighting one lamp, and writing page after page in longhand, fingers stiff with cold.

At first she could not understand any of this. Without drugs, she had never had such surges of energy. It must be the cold, she thought: adrenalin for survival. But after a few weeks she knew it was not the cold. It was the book, warming her from within, breathing life.

One night the space heater quit in exhaustion; it had never worked so hard for so long, she was sure. Dr. Foxx used it only on chilly nights in the early spring; it had been installed perhaps forty years ago. Had it ever been asked to keep anyone alive over such a winter? Impulsively she decided to clean its insides. Cleaning to stay alive, she told herself firmly, is different. She scoured ancient layers of burnt-on oil and rust, and put it back together. It sputtered relief, like a grateful Tin Woodsman, and paid her back at once, embracing her with a burst of heat. She smiled. Dear Mommy, Today I made my first friend at camp.

Sometimes she walked outside along the dirt path, or along the bay to pick up driftwood for the fire. Sometimes she biked to town to check the mail and see if people still lived here, selling food or toothpaste to other survivors. It always surprised her that they did. A car passing the house startled her now; she had grown as unaccustomed to the sound of cars as that of human voices. Possibly they were all around her, people and cars, but she was somewhere else, transported into another time, or a work of fiction.

Dr. Foxx wrote that he was coming out on April 1. She circled it on her calendar. Dr. Foxx due April 1, like fools and filers of early tax returns. He wrote that the telephone was being reconnected, and that she should remember to drain the space heater if it got warmer, and that he had a good feeling about coming out, knowing that she was there. The world is coming back, she reflected with mixed feelings. She had not finished being alone. She had not finished the book, either. Almost, but not quite.

She wrote fifteen pages on April 1, hurrying. Suddenly, at two o'clock, she found herself staring at the ashes in the fireplace, at the pile of blankets, the chaos of pillows on the floor. At three o'clock she shut off the typewriter and covered it. She put away the pens and the notebooks. Then she succumbed to an orgy of cleaning, the first in months. He had said he was leaving the city at two. It would take him less than two hours, even if traffic was heavy, even if he stopped at the roadside vegetable stands to check the prices of local zucchini this early in the season. That left her scarcely an hour to cover the traces of her game of solitaire. An hour to prepare, like a returning astronaut, for reentry and splashdown. She scrubbed, imagining him on the highway, speeding past Smithtown. She swept and dusted, imagining him approaching the turnoff to the William Floyd Parkway. She polished, feeling the crunch of his wheels on the dirt road outside the house. Hurry.

Chapter

FIFTEEN

IT WAS A record carload, even for him. He had scheduled the last patient for one o'clock, which would have given him fifteen minutes to pack and load and leave by two. But he was running six minutes late; his accountant called, with an urgent request for eighteen pieces of paper he had put somewhere and needed to find by Monday. He promised to take all his files out to the country and go through them over the weekend.

It was nearly one when he finished working, and absolutely nothing was ready. He packed according to his usual system; anything went, wherever it would fit. The first spring weekend, he could never remember what he had left out there last fall with deliberate foresight, so that he wouldn't have to duplicate it next April. Before closing the house, he always compiled a list: shaving cream, razor, tan corduroy pants, canned tomato paste. Then he would file the list neatly in a folder as soon as he got back to the city. But somehow the folder was missing every April; somehow he spent half an hour every April looking for it, and not finding it, and ending up taking another can of shaving cream, another razor, another pair of tan corduroy pants.

He threw books and bread into his tennis bag; pajamas and loose money into his attaché case; sneakers into the back seat; racquets into the front; cans of balls on the floor. The back seat was packed solid enough to block all rear vision; he would have to rely on the side mirror, which someone thoughtful had cracked for him last week. He was in such a hurry he almost forgot to empty the refrigerator. He had to take everything that ought to be eaten at once because it was already a borderline case: souring milk that could still be used for pancakes, aging rolls, greening bacon, dead lettuce. Everything into brown grocery bags; all the real bags were overflowing. Cuttings from four plants, carefully nurtured in jars of water; these went on the floor, tightly wedged; he would have to be careful about hitting bumps. The trunk of the car he saved for last. Three bulging shopping bags had to go in there, fitted around the spare tire and the rusty jack. Shoes and clothing first, as a kind of foundation. Then the bags—one of food, the other two crammed with every piece of paper that might conceivably pertain to last year's taxes.

Finally, under the driver's seat, today's mail and newspapers, plus the notes for an article on "male pre-menopausal tensions," which was three weeks overdue for *Medical Times*. He could polish it off on Sunday, after sorting the tax stuff, after tennis, after the Sunday paper, after . . .

The hood wouldn't close. He removed a jar containing the rest of this morning's cold coffee and the bag of food. Whatever didn't fit could share the front passenger seat with his jacket, sweaters, racquets and bedroom slippers. Done. He slammed the hood a second time and eased himself into the car, sweaty, disgruntled, half an hour late.

Once over the bridge and on the highway, in light traffic, his mood brightened. He began to think about the weekend and about seeing her. For once he would open the door of that house without wondering darkly whether the burglars had struck again. Four years ago they had broken in. Breaking into that house could be done with a pair of blunt safety scissors; possibly even a high note on a trumpet would do it. They took all the old copper pots he'd hung in the kitchen, and the pewter mugs, and the grandfather clock. They took the Boston rocker—the one antique he had personally added to the house. They had even taken the portrait of Daniel Webster. He could never understand why they had taken Daniel Webster and left Mark Twain. But every September thereafter, he had left two little notes to the burglars, one taped to the front door, one to the back, in case they thought he had bought another Boston rocker or set of copper pots: "There is nothing of value here any more, so please don't break in." Appealing to their tender hearts. For some reason he still thought burglars had tender hearts in eastern Long Island.

He wondered how the house would look, with her having lived there all this time. And how she would look. From her letters it seemed that she had thrived there and been happy.

He was making excellent time, nearing Little Neck, which he had always thought of, more aptly, as Bottleneck. It was all clear, and he settled back, accelerating; maybe he would make up the time, after all. He was going seventy when he hit the bump and the hood of the car flew open. It swung straight up against the windshield, blocking his whole view of the road. He braked gently, praying that no one was behind him or directly in front. He had to get over to the shoulder from the center lane, steering blind, signaling, praying, holding his breath, until he felt soft earth under him instead of road.

Made it. He exhaled, and sat there for a second, shaking with fright. Then he got out to survey the damage. The jars with the plants, of course; all the water spilled over the floor of the car. Drenched papers and clothes; nothing serious. He went to check the trunk. The attaché case was still tightly wedged, and the clothes, and the two shopping bags. A miracle. He heaved another ragged sigh and was about to close the hood when he noticed the papers flying over the road. No. He glanced again at the shopping bags: half empty. Those papers flying over the road—his tax records? His life? His canceled checks, bank statements, brokerage receipts, buys and sells,

patient account sheets? Every shred of substantiation
that he, S. Conrad Foxx, M.D., had existed at all
last year? They were whirling, dipping and fluttering overhead like migrating birds. It was a very windy
day.

He stood there a full minute, stunned, watching
the scraps, like bits of his own flesh, floating gaily
toward Utopia Parkway. A blizzard. A ticker-tape parade in honor of the returning hero. Then he began to
run. Darting back and forth across the road, dodging
cars, barely aware of them. Hey, look, some nut chas-
ing papers in the middle of the Long Island Expressway.

He raced the wind and the cars for almost an
hour. Crossing the parkway again and again, jogging
alongside, trying to guess where something might
land, trying to get there first. Occasionally he would
catch something and feel instant elation, like a center
fielder in his first varsity game. Sometimes he stood
still on the center island, craftily measuring the wind
velocity, plotting his moves before taking off. Yards
and yards he ran, pursuing a single check, a single
receipt. He would watch it dip, and would pounce
just as it took off again for somewhere else, plucked by
a new breeze. The other team—fate?—always sent in
a replacement without calling time.

His lungs were bursting. Looming over him was
the horrified face of his accountant. What? What? he
kept shouting in Foxx's inner ear. Then the face
would fade, replaced by the face of a small gray per-
sonage in serious glasses. An IRS auditor's face.
Bank statements? Well, you see . . . The auditor,

blue fluorescent lights gleaming on his glasses, eyes blank, uncomprehending. Or rather, comprehending all too well. No canceled checks for the year in question? I see.

It would be dark soon. He headed back to the car, a handful of salvaged papers clutched in his fist. His windfall. The wind would have been delighted to go on with the game, into overtime. Sudden death, it was called. He could still see legitimate deductions dancing tantalizingly over there, in the westbound lane. Maybe one more dash? No.

Maybe he should sit in the car awhile until the wind died down? In another half-hour he'd need a flashlight—and maybe an ambulance. No point. To be brutally realistic about it, there was no point in living at all after this. April Fool.

At five o'clock she stopped cleaning, like a factory hand at the blast of the whistle. She had been wiping things for two hours straight; the house would pass. She stared with distaste at her hands; dirt was embedded in all the cracks. She was too exhausted to work any more. At anything. She glanced guiltily at the typewriter, covered like a recent accident victim, then sat down near the window, listening with the ears of a hungry cat whose dinner hour has come and gone, and no sign yet of the master.

But *why?* She didn't understand. Why would he be doing this to her now? It made no sense at all. After six months he didn't need to prove that he was in no hurry to see her. But she was unconvincing and unconvinced. By six o'clock all the months of independence had vanished, and the last of her strength. She was a rejected child again, sobbing into pillows, waiting for him to care that she was waiting.

All the dull masochistic ache flooded back into its accustomed places—the insides of her wrists, the small of her back, the back of her neck, and most of all her groin. How long since she had last felt this special secret pain? Unlove. It had only been a minute; it had never really been away. She stared out into the gathering dark, hating him for reducing her, despising herself for having come so far, only to find that it was full circle, after all. The book lay unfinished on his old school desk. The woman sat unfinished at his window. April Fool.

At seven-ten she heard his car. It was nearly a quarter of a mile away, at the sharp turnoff near the gas station, but she could tell that it was him. She wished, oh, God, she wished there were a place to hide now, to run so that he would not find her rooted here like this. Dead, gone, lost in the woods, afloat in the melting bay, anywhere but not here, not waiting for him here like a spider.

Then he was standing in the doorway, framed in yellow light, a medieval portrait of a lesser martyr.

He had seen her from the dirt road, face pressed against the window, crazy nut, waiting for him in his crazy house. The two of them were still standing. He almost cried at the sight of them. Both beautiful. He had forgotten how he loved to look at her face when she wasn't crying."

"Hi," she said, that strange little catch in her voice. He knew the sound: tear warning.

Suddenly she saw the lines strung across his face, high-tension wires, and knew it had nothing to do with her.

"You'll never believe—" he began, hoarse with misery, and she ran to him, crushing her own silly pain against his. April Fools.

They walked out to the car, still entwined, while he told her what happened. She shook her head at the sight of the car swollen with his junk, spilling indigestible mouthfuls of it. She shook her head again, hearing him tell what had happened. Together they relieved the car of its burdens. She wanted to cry or to laugh, if he would only do either one with her.

Finally they came to the bag of food. She peered into it cautiously and found the dead lettuce. "All things considered," she said, removing it gently as though it were the hurt part of him, "I guess we'd better make a killing tomorrow at the vegetable stand." He smiled. Full of pain, yes, but God, she thought, that smile. Then came the laughter. Doubled-over, maniac laughter. It rolled over them, tumbling out like waves, like tears, like paper money in the wind. Laughter applied like kisses for healing. April Fool.

"Where is it?" he asked her later, meaning the book.

"Here," she said, presenting it to him, swaddled in its brown folder. "Everything but the ending."

"Does it have a name?"

"Yes," she said. "*My Turn.*"

He gave her a funny look. "Crazy," he said. She smiled.

The fire was nearly out; they had sat, huddled together in the wad of blankets, staring into it, fighting sleep. Small orange flecks still glowed on and off, like Mexican opals. She wanted to make love here, now, with it dying—soft stroboscopic flickering love. She reached behind him, pulling pillows off the sofa, piling them under their heads. Now they could lie together, still facing the fire. He stirred the last bits of wood carefully and lay beside her, pulling the blankets closer. "Cold," he said. "Not cold," she replied, taking off all three of her sweaters and pressing her body against him.

"Not cold," he agreed. He held her and stroked her back softly until she shivered. And then she took off her jeans too, and lay against him and kissed the curve of his neck above the collarbone, until he murmured something. "What?" she said. "Love you," he said.

She unsnapped his jeans. He slid them off, kicked them away and took off his sweater. The fire crackled applause. "Nice here," she said, curling against him, shifting so that he could touch both of her breasts, so that all of her body could move and open and take him in for the night. He murmured something, "Mmm" or "Ah," and kissed her in several nice places, and opened his eyes and smiled at her. She pushed the blankets away to watch their two bodies moving and flickering among the shadows, and then she moved down to taste more of him, slowly, making it last, like dessert. Tiny licks stretching it out, not too tiny, though, or you end up tasting mostly spoon, making the sweetness disappear too soon. Tasting, between his thighs, along his cock, inside him. Fitting her body to his, over it; he held her where she wanted to be, high, riding now, posting, a blue-ribbon rider feeling the wind, the sun, the double rhythm. Like horses. Like tap-dancing. Like making love. She felt him sigh, and then the rush of him inside her, the way a child sobs, she thought, in spite of itself.

She went on moving, slower now, the carousel winding down, music still crashing but slower, because the ride is almost over, the colors are clear now, not blurred and wild, and the rising and falling is slowing too. He was still inside her, warming, filling, waiting for the hidden sunbursts, the ring inside, flashing tiny golden lights like quills, like echoes, like circles from a falling pebble in a clear warm stream. Down and down, silent golden rings.

He felt her body close softly around him, a morning glory folding for the night. "I love you," he sighed, touching her mouth with the tips of his fingers. She tasted herself on them. "I wonder," she whispered against the fingers, "I wonder what he means by that."

"God knows," he said. "And Harry Stack Sullivan had a rough idea."

Dawn, the color of ashes, woke her first. An occasional spark flared fitfully in the dead fire, then snuffed itself out for lack of encouragement.

I should stir it, she thought. I should add more wood. So much hard work to keep the smallest fire alive. But in this cold, fragile house she had learned to husband any source of warmth; if need be, she could live without it. But she had also learned that need was never the whole story.

She curled against him, trying to seal off the cold spaces between their bodies. He made a soft sound, not quite a sigh, as her mouth grazed the back of his neck.

"Now that I can function," she whispered, "as a serious person—"

"Mmpf," he replied.

"I think I could call you—Sandor."

He rolled over to face her, eyes wide and blazing. In this light they were a clear green, like the stripe of a Hungarian flag. "No!" he said. "Absolutely no."

Her smile wavered, but she didn't flinch. "No?" she said. "Why not?"

"Because it's pronounced *Shan*-dor," he said, and grinned at her.

"*Shan*-dor," she echoed perfectly, and grinned back.

After a while, when he had closed his eyes again, she got up and tiptoed to the window with her notebook. He was smiling in his sleep when she began to write.

THE BIG BESTSELLERS
ARE AVON BOOKS!

Final Analysis Lois Gould	22343	$1.75
The Wanderers Richard Price	22350	$1.50
The Eye of the Storm Patrick White	21527	$1.95
Jane Dee Wells	21519	$1.75
Theophilus North Thornton Wilder	19059	$1.75
Daytime Affair Joshua Lorne	20743	$1.75
The Secret Life of Plants Peter Tompkins and Christopher Bird	19901	$1.95
The Wildest Heart Rosemary Rogers	20529	$1.75
Come Nineveh, Come Tyre Allen Drury	19026	$1.75
World Without End, Amen Jimmy Breslin	19042	$1.75
The Oath Elie Wiesel	19083	$1.75
A Different Woman Jane Howard	19075	$1.95
The Wolf and the Dove Kathleen E. Woodiwiss	18457	$1.75
Sweet Savage Love Rosemary Rogers	17988	$1.75
I'm OK—You're OK Thomas A. Harris, M.D.	14662	$1.95
Jonathan Livingston Seagull Richard Bach	14316	$1.50

Where better paperbacks are sold, or directly from the publisher. Include 25¢ per copy for mailing; allow three weeks for delivery. Avon Books, Mail Order Dept., 250 West 55th Street, New York, N.Y. 10019

BB2-75

THE BESTSELLER STARRING FICTION'S NEWEST, MOST ENGAGING HEROINE

Jane

A Novel by Dee Wells

"One of those books that one can't put down..."

The New York Times

She's thirty-four, carefree and single, an American journalist living in a London loft along with a cat, a vibrant sense of humor, and three carefully scheduled lovers: Tom is Tuesdays, Anthony is Thursdays, Franklin is weekends, and none of them knows about the others...until something comes into Jane's life that she hadn't counted on!

150,000 HARDCOVERS SOLD
SELECTED BY THE LITERARY GUILD

SOON A MAJOR MOTION PICTURE FROM COLUMBIA PICTURES

21519 / $1.75

J 1-75

AVON ⬥ THE BEST IN
BESTSELLING ENTERTAINMENT!

Facing the Lions Tom Wicker	19307	$1.75
Rule Britannia Daphne du Maurier	19547	$1.50
Play of Darkness Irving A. Greenfield	19077	$1.50
Sweet Savage Love Rosemary Rogers	17988	$1.75
High Empire Clyde M. Brundy	18994	$1.75
How You Can Profit from the Coming Devaluation Harry Browne	21972	$1.75
The Eiger Sanction Trevanian	15404	$1.75
The Flame and the Flower Kathleen E. Woodiwiss	22137	$1.75
Open Marriage Nena and George O'Neill	14084	$1.95
Gone With The Wind Margaret Mitchell	22319	$2.25
Between Parent and Child Dr. Haim G. Ginott	15677	$1.50
How I Found Freedom in an Unfree World Harry Browne	17772	$1.95
Zelda Nancy Milford	11536	$1.50